DOCTOR WH
INVASION

W9-CJC-649

## Also available in the Target series:

DOCTOR WHO AND THE ZARBI
DOCTOR WHO AND THE CRUSADERS
DOCTOR WHO AND THE AUTON INVASION
DOCTOR WHO AND THE CAVE-MONSTERS
DOCTOR WHO AND THE DAEMONS
DOCTOR WHO AND THE SEA-DEVILS
DOCTOR WHO AND THE CYBERMEN
DOCTOR WHO AND THE TERROR OF THE AUTONS
DOCTOR WHO AND THE CURSE OF PELADON
DOCTOR WHO AND THE ABOMINABLE SNOWMEN
DOCTOR WHO AND THE GREEN DEATH
DOCTOR WHO AND THE LOCH NESS MONSTER
DOCTOR WHO AND THE TENTH PLANET
DOCTOR WHO AND THE REVENGE OF THE CYBERMEN
DOCTOR WHO AND THE GENISIS OF THE DALEKS
DOCTOR WHO AND THE WEB OF FEAR
DOCTOR WHO AND THE SPACE WAR
DOCTOR WHO AND THE PLANET OF THE DALEKS
DOCTOR WHO AND THE PYRAMIDS OF MARS
DOCTOR WHO AND THE CARNIVAL OF MONSTERS
DOCTOR WHO AND THE SEEDS OF DOOM
DOCTOR WHO AND THE DALEK INVASION OF EARTH
DOCTOR WHO AND THE CLAWS OF AXOS
DOCTOR WHO AND THE ARK IN SPACE
DOCTOR WHO AND THE BRAIN OF MORBIUS
THE MAKING OF DOCTOR WHO
DOCTOR WHO AND THE PLANET OF EVIL
DOCTOR WHO AND THE MUTANTS
DOCTOR WHO AND THE DEADLY ASSASSIN
DOCTOR WHO AND THE TALONS OF WENG-CHIANG
DOCTOR WHO AND THE MASQUE OF MANDRAGORA
DOCTOR WHO AND THE FACE OF EVIL
DOCTOR WHO AND THE TOMB OF THE CYBERMEN
DOCTOR WHO AND THE TIME WARRIOR
DOCTOR WHO AND THE HORROR OF FANG ROCK
DOCTOR WHO—DEATH TO THE DALEKS
DOCTOR WHO AND THE ANDROID INVASION
DOCTOR WHO AND THE SONTARAN EXPERIMENT
DOCTOR WHO AND THE HAND OF FEAR
DOCTOR WHO AND THE INVISIBLE ENEMY
DOCTOR WHO AND THE ROBOTS OF DEATH
DOCTOR WHO AND THE IMAGE OF THE FENDAHL
DOCTOR WHO AND THE WAR GAMES
DOCTOR WHO AND THE DESTINY OF THE DALEKS
DOCTOR WHO AND THE RIBOS OPERATION
DOCTOR WHO AND THE UNDERWORLD

# DOCTOR WHO AND THE INVASION OF TIME

Based on the BBC television serial by David Agnew by arrangement with the British Broadcasting Corporation

## TERRANCE DICKS

A TARGET BOOK
*published by*
the Paperback Division of
W. H. Allen & Co. Ltd

A Target Book

Published in 1980
by the Paperback Division of W. H. Allen & Co. Ltd
A Howard & Wyndham Company
44 Hill Street, London W1X 8LB

Copyright © 1979 by Terrance Dicks and David Agnew
'Doctor Who' series copyright © 1979 by the British
Broadcasting Corporation

Printed in Great Britain by
Richard Clay (The Chaucer Press) Ltd, Bungay, Suffolk

ISBN 0 426 20093 4

# Contents

# 1

## Treaty for Treason

The space ship was enormous, terrifying, a long, sleek killer-whale of space. Its hull-lines were sharp and predatory and it bristled with the weapon-ports of a variety of death dealing devices. Everything about it suggested devastating, murderous power.

It was the flag-ship of the Vardan war fleet, heading towards a planet called Gallifrey.

Inside the space ship was another of even more advanced design, though it would have been difficult to tell as much from the outside. It took the form of a square blue police box, of the kind once used on the planet Earth. Inside was an impossibly large control room. The craft was called the TARDIS, and it was dimensionally transcendental, bigger on the inside than on the outside.

The control room held a many-sided central console and two people, or to be strictly accurate, one female humanoid and one automaton.

The human was a girl called Leela. She was tall and strong, with brown eyes and long reddish-brown hair, and she wore a brief costume of animal skins with a fighting knife at the belt. She paced up and down the control room like a great cat. Leela was a primitive, a savage, raised as a fighting warrior in a tribe called the Sevateem.

The automaton was shaped like a robot dog, and was appropriately called K9. Both were companions of that mysterious traveller in space and time known

7

as the Doctor, and both were wondering what had become of him.

The Doctor's behaviour tended to be odd and arbitrary at the best of times, but recently he had excelled himself.

To begin with he had fallen into a strange, abstracted mood, silent for long periods, answering questions with brief, snappish replies. He seemed to be listening much of the time, staring abstractedly into space like someone straining to catch a faint message on the edge of hearing.

The strange mood had ended in a flurry of equally mysterious activity. The Doctor had hunched himself over the control board and punched a long and complex series of co-ordinates into the navigation circuits, correcting and re-correcting as if determined to arrive at some utterly precise destination in space and time. And now here they were inside an enormous alien space ship. The Doctor had checked their arrival co-ordinates, given a grunt of satisfaction, ordered them not to touch the scanner, and marched straight out of the control room without a word of explanation.

Leela and K9 were left to wait—and wonder.


In the war room of the Vardan flag-ship, an enormous screen took up the whole of one wall. On the screen, against a backdrop of stars, was a visual display of the Vardan battle fleet, squadron upon squadron in the typical Vardan V-formation, heading remorselessly towards Gallifrey.

Studying the display stood a tall, strangely-dressed figure. He wore loose and comfortable-looking clothes with a vaguely Bohemian air. An immensely long multi-coloured scarf was wound about his neck, a

8

battered broad-brimmed soft hat was jammed onto a tangle of curly hair.

There was a long curved conference table below the screen, and behind the table high-backed chairs held the members of the Vardan war council. An ornate, elaborately-sealed document lay in the centre of the table.

The Vardan Leader spoke in a thin, impatient voice. 'Speed is vital, Doctor. Sign!'

Leela completed yet another circuit of the control room, stopped and stared impatiently down at K9. 'How much longer is he going to be?'

'Prognostication in matters concerning the Doctor impossible.'

'Prog-what?'

'I cannot tell.'

'Can you tell me where we are then?'

'Affirmative.'

'Well?'

'Materialisation has taken place inside an alien space craft.'

'Why wouldn't the Doctor let me go with him?'

'I do not know. Prognostication in matters concerning the Doctor is——'

'Impossible!' completed Leela. 'I know ... but he may need help.' Leela was quite convinced that the Doctor was far too impractical to take care of himself. 'I'm going to take a look at the scanner.'

'Do not touch scanner control, Mistress.'

'I know the Doctor said we shouldn't ... but wouldn't you like to see what he's doing, K9, who he's talking to?'

'Negative. Curiosity is an emotion. I am not pro-grammed for emotion.'

9

'Oh shut up,' said Leela crossly. 'You're no help at all.' She turned on the scanner. Nothing happened. 'What's wrong? Why won't it work?' She flicked the switch impatiently. 'Why?' K9 didn't answer. Leela looked down. 'K9 sulking's emotional behaviour too, you know. If you cannot be curious, then you cannot sulk.'

More silence.

'K9, I'm sorry,' said Leela cajolingly. 'I didn't mean to shout at you.'

'Apologies are not necessary,' said K9, but his tail antenna was wagging gently.

Leela smiled. 'No, of course not. Now, can you please tell me why the scanner will not work?'

'The Doctor immobilised the mechanism before he left.'

'He doesn't trust me!' said Leela indignantly. 'What's he *doing* out there?'


'It is time to conclude these formalities, Doctor,' said the Vardan leader impatiently. 'Sign the treaty!'

The Doctor swung round. 'I never sign anything before I read it.'

'Then read!'

The Doctor picked up the document and scanned it rapidly. 'You promised me complete control over the Time Lords.'

'You will have complete control.'

'But in paragraph four subsection three, it states that——'

'Mere lawyers' quibbles, Doctor.'

'I've heard that one before,' said the Doctor suspiciously. 'Lawyers' quibbles can get you killed.'

'Sign it.'

The Doctor sighed. 'Oh well, I've signed so many

10

things in my lives ... one more won't make any difference.'

'But it will,' said the Vardan softly. 'It will!'

The Doctor produced an old-fashioned fountain pen from his pocket. '*Complete* control?'

'My word on it.'

The Doctor scrawled an elaborate set of hieroglyphics across the bottom of the document, straightened up, and bowed elaborately. 'I am honoured to serve the glorious Vardan cause.'

A few minutes later the Doctor was being greeted with a barrage of questions from Leela.

'Doctor, where have you been? What have you been doing? What's going on?'

'Sssh!' said the Doctor. He went straight over to the control console and began punching up coordinates.

'Doctor, where have you *been*?'

'Order K9 to tell you to shut up!'

'K9 tell me to shut up? How dare you!'

Taking Leela's repetition as an order, K9 glided over to her. 'Please adopt silent mode, Mistress.'

'Now look here, K9 ...'

The blaster extruded from beneath K9's nose. 'Imperative, Mistress.'

Leela knew the blaster would only be set on stun, but being stunned by K9 was quite an unpleasant experience.

Leela shut up.

The Castellan's new suite of offices was an elaborate affair of transparent plastic and gleaming metal, with complex control consoles and brightly flickering vision

11

screens everywhere. It was over-technological even by Time Lord standards, but Kelner, the new Castellan felt it helped to maintain his image. (The newly-formed Castellan's Bodyguard Squad served the same purpose) Kelner was a thin-faced, nervous, rather insecure Time Lord who owed his position to a combination of good birth and political intrigue.

Spandrel the previous Castellan, now retired, had been content with shabby chambers in an old, run down quarter of the Capitol. But then, Spandrel had been a tough, no nonsense character, who felt no need to keep up appearances. Kelner was very different.

The new Castellan sat behind an enormous desk in his inner sanctum. The outer offices held his various assistants. Chief among them was a handsome young Time Lord called Andred, Commander of the Chancellery Guard. Andred was seldom to be found at his desk. He didn't much care for Kelner, and took good care that his various duties kept him out and about in the enormous sprawling Capitol, the city-sized complex of buildings that was the seat of all Time Lord government.

At this particular moment Andred was at his desk for once, which was fortunate since an urgent and alarming message had just arrived.

Andred was impatiently demanding further details from the speaker on the other end of the communications circuit. 'Speak up, man. Where? When—no *relative* time, fool! Thank you!' Andred sat frowning for a moment. Much as he loved the grandeur of his position, Castellan Kelner didn't really like to be troubled with actual work. He would reprove you for bothering him with trivia—and complain even more savagely if he wasn't told everything he needed to know. Andred rose, and went into the inner office.

Gorgeous in Castellan's robes, Kelner sat gazing

into space, presumably contemplating his own importance.

Andred coughed and Kelner seemed to become aware of his presence. 'Yes, what is it, Commander?'

'A report has just come in, sir.'

'Continue.'

'Temporal scan has just picked up an unidentified capsule approaching Gallifrey.'

'Unidentified?' Kelner was displeased. Everything on Gallifrey had to be identified, docketed, regulated. An unidentified capsule was against all the rules.

'At this distance, within our own Continum, the capsule, is still unidentified.'

'But it *is* one of our own?'

'Long-range scan of molecular patina seems to indicate Gallifreyan origin,' said Andred cautiously. 'But it's still too early for a positive identification.'

'Present defence level?'

'Still on Green, sir.'

'No sense in taking chances, Commander. Go to Amber.'

'Yes sir. I'll need the code-key, sir.'

There was a structure of multicoloured globes on Kelner's desk, rather like a laboratory model of an atom. Kelner took one of the little globes from its setting and handed it to Andred.

Andred took the globe and left the office. Returning to his own control complex, he held the globe before a scanner. 'Main security? Commander Andred speaking. Please establish Amber Alert immediately.'

There was a brief musical bleep from the console as the command code was recorded and accepted.


The Doctor and K9 were alone in the control room. Leela had gone off in a huff.

13

The Doctor was studying his control console. 'They've put an Amber Alert on me! An Amber Alert! Cheek!'

K9 was baffled. He wasn't programmed for slang. 'Cheek, Master?'

'Yes, cheek!'

'Cheek ... physical characteristics ... humanoid facial component.'

'Wrong,' said the Doctor absently.

K9 whirred and clicked. 'Data check insists definition correct.'

The Doctor ignored him. 'An Amber Alert, eh?'

It wasn't clear if he thought the degree of alarm was too severe, or not severe enough.


'We have confirmation now, sir,' reported Andred. 'The capsule is definitely Gallifreyan.'

'Then what is all the fuss about?'

'It's still unidentified, sir.'

Kelner punched a control panel and a set of symbols appeared on the readout screen of his desk computer. 'Only two Time Lords are currently absent on authorised research. If you check their molecular codings ...'

'I've already done that, sir. Neither of them match.'

Kelner rubbed long, bony hands together in alarm. 'Then who is in that capsule? Unauthorised use of a Time Capsule carries the death penalty, Commander. See to it!'

Andred went back to his console. 'Commander Andred to all Guard Leaders. An unidentified capsule is approaching the Capitol.' He paused, formulating his orders. 'If there is no sign of life, the capsule will be destroyed on materialisation. If a sentient life-form emerges, arrest and hold for interrogation.' Andred paused. 'If the alien resists arrest—kill him!'

14

## 2

## The President-Elect

'Like a dog-biscuit, K9,' said the Doctor suddenly. 'Or a ball-bearing?'

K9 was hurt. 'Please do not mock me, Master.'

'Where's Leela?'

'Immersed, Master.'

'What?'

'Totally immersed in $H_2O$, Master.'

'This is a fine time to take a bath!' said the Doctor indignantly. 'That girl's got no sense of occasion.'

Leela swam to and fro in a luxurious swimming pool that was only one of the TARDIS's many surprises. Since it was dimensionally transcendental, the interior of the TARDIS was virtually limitless in size. Leela had discovered the swimming pool on one of her trips of exploration, to the astonishment of the Doctor who had completely forgotten it was there. She used it often now, especially when she was worried. It seemed the nearest thing the TARDIS could provide to the open air.

Leela was worried now, as she swam length after length with smooth, powerful strokes. The Doctor's strange behaviour seemed to be getting steadily worse. She couldn't shake off the feeling that he was heading blindly into terrible danger. Climbing out of the pool, she shook herself dry and went to find him.

Andred paused at the entrance to the Castellan's office. 'They've estimated the landing place of the capsule, sir. Right in the heart of the Capitol. I think I'll go and supervise its destruction personally.'

Kelner waved him away. 'Of course. And remember, Andred, an alien who can steal and control a capsule is dangerous by definition. He is to be captured, interrogated, and then executed.'

'I will see that all the regulations are observed, sir,' Andred stiffly replied, and marched away.


In the war room of their flag-ship, members of the Vardan council were studying a complex flickering of symbols on a video screen. 'Interesting,' said the Leader softly. 'He appears to have landed.'

One of the council said dubiously, 'Perhaps they will kill him at once.'

'No matter. There will be others . . .'


The TARDIS appeared at the bottom of a flight of steps in one of the ante-chambers of the main Capitol building. The choice of arrival point was a worrying one, decided Andred. The Chancellor's office was very close.

The moment it materialised the TARDIS was surrounded by a squad of Chancellery Guards. They waited, tense and alert, stasers trained on the blue box.

The TARDIS door opened and the Doctor strode out.

He stared arrogantly about him, suddenly appeared to notice the guards and favoured them with a lordly wave. 'Well, hello, gentlemen. It *is* nice to be back!'

Andred gave a signal, and the guards brought their stasers to their shoulders.

The Doctor beamed. 'Good, very good. I like to see a smart bit of drill!' He strode up to the nearest guard like some visiting general. 'And where are you from, my man?'

There was just the right note of jovial authority in his voice and the guard answered automatically. 'Gallifrey, sir.'

'Gallifrey, eh?' said the Doctor thoughtfully. 'Never heard of it!'

He strolled down the line and stopped in front of another guard. Before anyone could stop him he snatched the man's staser, peered down the muzzle, then threw the weapon back to him. 'Disgusting, absolutely filthy!' He raked the line of guards with a withering stare. 'Call yourselves an Honour Guard? Disgraceful, a rabble that's all you are, a rabble, not fit to guard a jelly baby!' With a sudden change of mood, the Doctor fished a crumpled paper bag from his pocket and offered it to the nearest guard. 'Would you care for a jelly baby, by the way?'

Andred came forward. Somehow the situation was getting out of his control. 'I don't think you understand, we're here to arrest you ...'

His voice tailed away, as he caught sight of Leela, who had suddenly appeared in the TARDIS doorway. He stood staring at her open-mouthed.

'Good, good,' said the Doctor cheerfully, and he strode towards the door. 'Let's get on with it, shall we?'

He set off at a brisk pace, and Leela started to follow him.

The Doctor whirled round. 'Where do you think you're going? You stay here till I send for you!'

Baffled and resentful, Leela stayed where she was, and the Doctor disappeared.

Andred hurried after him. 'Number one section

17

with me, number two, guard the girl.' Leela was left standing beside the TARDIS. The guards closed in on her.

The Doctor strode through the wide marble corridors of the chancellery, Andred hurrying to catch up with him. 'Halt!' shouted Andred.

The Doctor stopped so suddenly that Andred nearly bumped into him.

'Right you are. Lead the way!'

'Follow me!' ordered Andred, determined to show who was in charge.

'Right,' said the Doctor amiably, and they went on their way.

The Doctor glanced from side to side as they walked along. Much of the Chancellery had been destroyed in the events of his last visit, but it had all been rebuilt by now, and in an even more elaborate style. 'Thing's have changed a bit since I was last here,' he said chattily, and came to a sudden halt outside a heavy, ornately carved door. 'Ah, here we are.'

Andred stared at him. 'That's the Chancellor's office.'

'I know!'

The Doctor moved towards the door, but Andred barred his way. 'No one can go in there unannounced.'

'Then announce me!'

Such was the authority in the Doctor's voice that Andred heard himself saying, 'Very well.'

He opened the door and went into the office. It was a long, high-ceilinged room, richly but simply furnished. Behind a huge desk at the far end sat a tall hawk-faced old man in the robes of a Cardinal, reading an ancient scroll. His face was seamed and wrinkled and his hair snowy white, but his back was straight and his eyes bright with intelligence.

This was Cardinal Borusa, now the most powerful

18

Time Lord on Gallifrey. Since the assassination of the last President by the last Chancellor, Borusa had been both Chancellor and Acting-President, until such time as a suitable Candidate for the Presidency could be found. That had been some time ago, but as yet no suitable candidate had appeared.

Borusa looked up, displeased at the interruption. 'Well?'

'Forgive the intrusion, sir, an unexpected emergency.'

The Doctor strode into the room, brushing Andred aside.

Borusa rose and to Andred's astonishment he actually smiled, holding out his arms in welcome. 'Doctor! What brings you back to Gallifrey?'

There was no answering smile on the Doctor's face. 'I am here to claim my legal right.'

'What right?'

'I claim the Inheritance of Rassilon. I claim the titles and honours, the duty and obedience of all colleges. I claim the Presidency of the High Council of the Time Lords.'

Far away in deep space, the War Leader of the Vardans looked up from the symbol-covered video-screen, dancing with its intricately patterned shapes ... 'I believe we have chosen well.'

K9 glided to and fro before the TARDIS console. 'Where is the Doctor?' he demanded.

There was no reply. The TARDIS console, usually throbbing with life was silent, dead.

'You are a very *stupid* machine,' said K9 reprovingly, and resumed his patrol.

Andred and the guards had been dismissed, and the Doctor and Borusa were alone.

'You do not dispute my claim?'

The old man looked sadly at his former pupil. The Doctor had always been a secret favourite of his, despite a tendency to rashness and indiscipline. Now he seemed to have slipped over the border between eccentricity and madness. 'I do not dispute the claim, only the lunatic arrogance with which it has been presented.'

'Still the pedant, eh, Borusa. How you used to bore me when I was at the Academy. All those endless lectures on responsibility and duty ...'

'Which obviously failed to make the slightest impression.'

'You taught me nothing. Nothing that instinct could not provide better.'

'Then you must trust your instincts.'

The Doctor looked strangely at him. 'Yes ... And you yours, Borusa.'

There was an odd little silence.

Borusa said wearily. 'Very well, I will do my best to persuade the other Cardinals to accept you as President.'

'I *am* the President,' said the Doctor with simple arrogance. 'No persuasion is needed.'

'Politeness dictates ...' began Borusa.

The Doctor interrupted him. '*Is* there another candidate—legally?'

'No. It was an unfortunate oversight.'

'Thank you!'

'I intended no disrespect.'

'Oh yes you did! Borusa, before you go, I need another lesson.'

'On what particular subject?'

20

'On the Constitution.'

'You had that at your fingertips, the last time we met.'

'And if I hadn't, you would have killed me.'

Borusa winced at the Doctor's accusation. There was an uncomfortable amount of truth in it. 'Not I, but the one who was then Chancellor . . .' he said defensively.

The Doctor's previous visit to Gallifrey, the first since he had fled into exile many long years before, had been brought about by the machinations of the Master, his greatest enemy. The Master had assassinated the President of Gallifrey and fixed the guilt of the murder upon the Doctor.

To escape execution, the Doctor had announced his candidacy for the Presidency, putting himself beyond the reach of the law. At the time this had simply been a legalistic device, to give the Doctor time to discover and unmask the real criminal. Nevertheless the Doctor *had* been accepted as a candidate for the Presidency, the only opposition candidate was now dead, and no other candidate had ever been brought forward. According to the ancient Constitution of Gallifrey, the Presidency had therefore passed to the Doctor by default.

'I stand corrected,' said the Doctor. 'The Chancellor would have killed me. Did you simply assume his post after his death?'

Borusa flushed angrily. 'The Council ratified my appointment.'

'Without a President, the Council can ratify nothing.'

'There *was* no President,' snapped Borusa. 'You were President-elect, it is true—but you chose to leave Gallifrey.'

'And now I have returned as President!' Borusa turned to leave and the Doctor snapped, 'A point which seems to have escaped you, Borusa. You haven't been given leave to depart.'

'Until you have been confirmed and inducted as President, I do not need your leave to do anything!'

'Then the ceremony had better take place at once.'

'It will be arranged as soon as possible——'

'*At once*,' repeated the Doctor implacably.

Borusa was too furious to speak. He inclined his head in the merest suggestion of a bow, turned and walked away.

A picture of lunatic grandeur, the Doctor leaned back in his chair and smiled.


With total absorption, the Vardan council studied the tracery of elaborate symbols on their vision screen.

'An interesting encounter,' hissed the Leader. 'Perhaps we should reconsider our plans for the Doctor. This needs thought.'

'The plan has been made,' objected one of the council. 'Our course has already been decided.'

'I may reconsider,' said the War Leader arrogantly. 'The Doctor seems to understand discipline. He could be useful to us. Perhaps we should not kill him after all...'

# 3

## Attack from the Matrix

'No discipline,' stormed Borusa. 'That has always been the Doctor's trouble.'

The Doctor's orders meant that an induction ceremony had to be arranged with almost indecent haste, and Borusa had come to consult with Kelner.

The Castellan had listened to the old man's angry recital with noncommittal calm. Kelner was first and foremost a politician. The new President, for all his eccentricities, seemed to be a man of purpose and decision, and, perhaps Borusa's day was already over. Kelner had no intention of allying himself with the losing side. 'Does the President-Elect fully understand the dangers? Does he accept the risk of induction into the Matrix without the necessary period of preparation?'

'He understands nothing, he accepts nothing.'

'No discipline!'

Andred came in and bowed to his two superiors. 'Forgive me, sirs, but the President-Elect desires your immediate attendance.'

'Then let him rot in the heart of a black star!' snarled Borusa.

'It is his urgent request, sir,' said Andred steadily. As if by accident, his hand touched the butt of his staser pistol. Commander Andred was a soldier, with a soldiers's loyalties. His duty was to serve the ruler of his planet, and as far as he understood it, that ruler was now the Doctor.

'A request is a request,' said Kelner smoothly. 'After all, Chancellor, it is only a matter of time before the President-Elect is confirmed in his authority.'

The Doctor received them in the Chancellor's office, still in his mood of manic jollity. He listened with approval to Borusa's report; the arrangements for the ceremony had been put in hand. 'Only a matter of time, then, gentlemen. Still it's always a matter of time, Castellan, especially for Time Lords.'

Borusa snorted. Kelner smiled humbly at the President-Elect's little joke.

'Now then,' said the Doctor cheerfully. 'About my office . . .'

'Simply a matter of a few formalities, sir,' said Kelner hurriedly.

'Oh, I know that. I don't mean the office of President, I mean my office, my quarters. You know, a room to sit and think in, somewhere to go when I want to be alone.' He looked disdainfully around him. 'I do so hate all this—squatting.'

'There are of course the previous Presidents quarters said Borusa acidly. 'He was a man of simple tastes, however. You might not find them adequate.'

The Doctor waved a hand. 'Then we must have them re-furnished.'

'In what style, sir?' asked Kelner.

Before the Doctor could reply, Borusa said angrily. 'May I remind you that we are not your lackeys? We are Time Lords. I am Chancellor——'

'Illegally!'

'I am a Cardinal, then. That, at least!'

'Oh yes,' agreed the Doctor contemptuously. 'That, at least. Now, take me to my office.'

The office of the President adjoined the Chancellor's, and a few moments later, Kelner was ushering the Doctor inside. The rooms, as Borusa had said, were

24

simply, almost sparsely furnished, carved tables, a couch or two, a few ancient tapestries.

'Oh no, this won't do at all,' said the Doctor. 'Still, the room has possibilities, I suppose. It will have to be completely redecorated of course.'

'Of course, sir,' agreed Kelner. 'Which style would you prefer?'

The Doctor gazed round the spacious room. 'Oh, I don't know. Early Quasar Five? A touch of Riga?'

'The merest hint of the Sinan Empire?' suggested Kelner.

'Second Dynasty, of course.'

'Of course, sir,' agreed Kelner.

Borusa said disgustedly. 'Why not Earth, Twentieth Century? I understand you've spent a good deal of time there?'

'Well, yes, I did get used to the place. Even liked it at times.'

Kelner converted the date Borusa had mentioned into Time Lord reckoning. 'Now let me see—that would be Sol Three ... Relative date zero point three four one seven three nine eight nine.'

'On second thoughts, I think I'd prefer the style of the old Thesaurian Empire—zero seven three, I think, the time when there was all that wonderful lead panelling. It was their rarest metal, you know, the equivalent of gold on Earth.'

Kelner bowed. 'But of course, sir.'

'Thank you,' said the Doctor graciously.

'It will take a little time, I'm afraid.'

'Oh, we've plenty of that.' The Doctor glanced at Borusa. 'Eh, Cardinal—I mean Chancellor—Elect.'

Kelner bowed. 'Will that be all, sir?'

'No. See to my friend Leela. Have her released, give her comfortable quarters, and suitable dress for my initiation ceremony. I shall expect her to attend.'

25

'Yes of course, sir.'

Kelner bowed his way out.

'May I also leave, President-Elect?' asked Borusa coldly.

'No. We have things to discuss.'

'What things?'

'The redecoration, for instance.'

'I'm sure the Castellan is quite capable of dealing with that.'

'Oh, yes, quite. But I would be grateful if you could supervise certain important details. The good Castellan has flaws in his understanding, does he not?'

Borusa gave the Doctor a sudden thoughtful look, but said nothing.

'For instance,' continued the Doctor, 'his knowledge hardly extends to the characteristic Thesaurian style of the zero seven three era.'

'Zero seven three?'

'Yes, you remember, all those marvellous lead panels. Very primitive, of course, but so effective.'

'Lead is a very difficult substance to control ...'

'Very few have mastered the art.'

'Then more must do so. Put your best craftsmen on it—immediately.'

'Where would you like the lead panels to be placed?'

'Everywhere, Borusa,' said the Doctor expansively.

'Everywhere?'

'Yes!' The Doctor swept his hand round the room in an extravagant gesture. 'Door, walls, ceiling, floor— *everywhere*!'


Leela held up an elaborate gold lamé robe and studied it disgustedly.

'That looks very good,' said Andred encouragingly.

26

Leela crumpled the elegant robe and tossed it to the floor.

Commander Andred sighed. 'Madam, please ...'

'My name is Leela.'

'Leela, we have tried every style of female attire in the entire cosmos. May I ask what you would like?'

'I would like a quiver of arrows, a bow, a pouch of Janis thorns, and my knife back.'

She reached for her knife, which was thrust into Andred's belt, but Andred caught her wrist and forced her hand away—not without effort, since she was almost as strong as he was. For a moment they stood locked in opposition, then Andred put forth his full strength and thrust her hand down and away. 'Madam —Leela,' he said deliberately, 'I have told you many times that I cannot give you back your knife. My guards were quite right to take it from you. All weapons are forbidden here, except for those carried by the guards themselves, for internal security.'

'You said the Doctor ordered you to look after me.'

'Yes, those were the President-Elect's instructions, Madam.'

In fact they had been Kelner's, passed on from the Doctor. Andred had accepted the assignment with mixed feelings. It meant that he would be seeing more of Leela, who was so much more vital and alive than the cool, remote Time Ladies one saw in the Capitol. Her savage beauty had made a considerable impression on Andred. But he hadn't been prepared for her fiercely independent temperament, and he felt as if he had been suddenly put in charge of a female wildcat. Leela had been unimpressed by the luxuriously furnished rooms he had provided for her. Now she was rejecting all his attempts to provide her with a more suitable wardrobe.

27

'I am sorry, Madam,' he began again.

'Don't call me Madam!'

'I am sorry, Leela, but I cannot give you your weapon.'

Leela grabbed a box of priceless jewels and threw them across the room. 'Then keep your fine clothes and useless baubles—and keep your President-Elect!'

In the Chancellor's office, Borusa was finishing an account of the long and complex ceremony that lay before the Doctor. 'And then Gold Usher will formally introduce you to the Matrix.'

'Just the Matrix,' asked the Doctor idly—but his eyes were bright with concentration.

'There is no *just* about it. The Matrix is—everything! The sum total of all the information that has ever been stored, that ever can be stored ... the imprints of the personalities of generations of Time Lords and their Presidents—their elected Presidents—will become available to you. It will become part of you, as you will become part of it.'

'Yes,' said the Doctor slowly. 'That's what I thought...'

(The Vardan Leader watched the swirling coalescence of symbols on his screen and said, 'Prepare!')

'But you know all this already,' said Borusa. 'Once before you have entered into the Amplified Panatropic Computer.'

'Yes ... I didn't like it much.' The Doctor had only been able to defeat the Master's murderous schemes by linking his mind with the APC net. In doing so,

28

he had entered a nightmare world, created by the rebel Time Lord who had been the Master's pawn. It was an experience that had almost cost the Doctor his sanity and his life.

'The APC net is only a small part of the Matrix,' said Borusa warningly. The psychic shock of union with the Matrix was considerable, and most Presidents-Elect prepared themselves for the ordeal with a long period of mental training. It was typical of the Doctor, thought Borusa, that he was prepared to take the risk with no preparation at all.

The Doctor said musingly. 'And when I have been introduced to the Matrix, I will have complete power?'

'More power than anyone in the known universe.'

'I'll put it to good use—the best use!'

'That is no more than your duty.'

The Doctor smiled. 'Oh yes, quite so, Borusa. Quite so!'

The Vardan War Leader rose. 'Summon the Commanders!'

'Full Alert?'

'Not yet. But the first phase is already nearing completion. We must be ready.'

Andred appeared in the doorway of Leela's chambers. 'Please come now, Leela it is time. You'll be late for the ceremony.'

Leela stood in the centre of the room, arms folded. 'I will not come unless you return my weapon.'

Andred sighed. He took the knife from his belt and passed it to Leela. She slipped it back into the sheath. 'This ceremony—it does the Doctor much honour?'

'The highest honour that our race can give.'

29

'Then I shall not let him down.' Leela remembered the complex ceremonies with which her own tribe marked the creation of a new chief. 'Are there duties for me? Rites I must observe, things I must do or not do?'

'There is nothing for you to do but attend and observe,' Andred paused. 'Oh, perhaps there is one thing, Leela?'

'Yes?'

'It would assist the smooth progress of the affair if you could refrain from killing anyone while the ceremony is in progress.'

'I will try,' promised Leela solemnly. She followed Andred from the room.

The grand hall of the Panopticon is an immense circular chamber used by the Time Lords for all their major ceremonies. It is one of the largest and most impressive chambers in the known universe. The immense marble floor is big enough to hold an army, the domed glass roof seems as high above as the sky itself. Row upon row of viewing galleries run around the walls, and on the far side of the hall an impressive staircase leads down to a raised circular dais. By now the hall was filled with rank upon rank of Time Lords, all wearing the different-coloured robes and insignia of the different Chapters, the complex social family and political organisations that dominated Time Lord Society.

As the hall slowly filled two very old, very eminent Time Lords stood close to the dais.

'Undue haste is bad enough,' said Lord Gomer pettishly. 'Vulgar bad manners is if anything possibly worse. Why, normally it takes years to discuss a Presidential Ordination let alone actually assemble one.'

Gomer was the Surgeon-General, a man of rigidly old-fashioned views.

Lord Savar nodded wisely. 'Unsettled times, eh, Gomer? Still, they say the time will throw up the man.'

'They say time brings wisdom too,' snapped Gomer. He stared pointedly at his ancient colleague. 'Incidentally, aren't you overdue for another regeneration?'

Savar ignored the remark. 'I believe I have wisdom to fit my years,' he said complacently.

'Just so, my lord,' said Gomer dryly. 'Ever hear of cyclic burst?'

'I beg your pardon?'

'The answer to many scientific problems may lie in the cyclic burst ratio,' said Gomer solemnly.

'The Black Star protect us! What is a cyclic burst ratio?'

'Oh, it's just a little study of mine, a hobby. You do understand what a hobby is?'

'I may have come across the term,' said Savar loftily. 'But I fail to understand any significant meaning.'

'That does not surprise me,' said Gomer dryly. Savar was not known for any unnecessary mental activity. Gomer persisted with his explanation, without much hope of being understood. 'I'm making a study of what I call wavelength broadcast power transduction.'

Savar covered a yawn. 'Really?'

'I've noticed lately, say over the last decade or so, an enormous fluctuation in relative wavelength transduction over a particularly narrow band ...'

To Savar's enormous relief, a fanfare of trumpets announced the arrival of the President-Elect.

Impressive in his long white robes the Doctor came down the great staircase and took his place on the central dais. Behind him came the appropriately robed Gold Usher, and behind him Castellan Kelner, High

31

Cardinal Borusa, and the other Cardinals and officials.

The Doctor took his place on the centre of the raised circular dais and the others grouped themselves formally around him.

Andred had found a place for Leela in the very front rank of the spectators. She was impressed in spite of herself, with the immense size of the hall, and the ornately robed crowd. These Time Lords must be a powerful tribe. The Doctor seemed a stranger in his long white ceremonial robes, his usually cheerful features cold and hard. His eyes flicked briefly, but without recognition, over Leela in her place in the front rank.

Gold Usher came to the front of the dais and held up his hand. There was total silence in the enormous hall.

He began to speak, declaiming his words in a sonorous rolling chant. 'Honoured members of the High Council, Cardinals, Time Lords ... Madam ...' He inclined his head briefly towards Leela, and for a moment there seemed a twinkle in his eye. Then the deep voice took up its impressive chant. 'We are here today to honour the will and the wisdom of Rassilon...'

('We are near victory,' hissed the Vardan War Chief, his eyes fixed on the screen.)

Leela's eyes glazed and her head nodded as the ceremony went on and on. Other Time Lords came forward and played their part, there were solemn incantations and responses, and what seemed like a recital of the entire history of the Time Lords. Finally Gold Usher came forward once more. Leela sensed that the ceremony was nearing its end. Gold Usher's ceremonial staff crashed down, the sound echoing thunderously. 'Is there anyone here to contest the right of the candidate to the Great Key of Rassilon?'

Again that total silence fell on the vast crowded hall.

'By custom, I shall strike three times. Should no voice be heard by the third stroke, I shall in duty bound, invest the candidate as President of the High Council of the Time Lords of Gallifrey.' The staff crashed down. Once ... twice ... The pauses between the echoing reverberations seemed endless.

('Now we have them,' hissed the Vardan War Leader exultantly.) The staff crashed down for the third time, and the echoes rolled away around the edges of the great hall. Gold Usher turned to the Doctor. 'It is my duty and privilege, by consent of the Time Lords of Gallifrey, to invest you as President of the High Council. Accept therefore the sash of Rassilon ...' Gold Usher took the heavy, ornate sash from a waiting guard and fastened it about the Doctor's shoulders.

'Accept therefore the Rod of Rassilon ...'

He placed a slender metal wand in the Doctor's hands.

'Seek, therefore to find the Great Key of Rassilon ...'

He gestured towards an empty cushion, held by another guard. (The Key of Rassilon had been stolen by the Master, and he had escaped with it after the failure of his attempt to destroy Gallifrey.)

The Doctor reached out his hand and touched the cushion in a ceremonial gesture.

'Do you swear to uphold the laws of Gallifrey? Do you swear to follow in the wisdom of Rassilon?'

'I swear.'

Another pause. Gold Usher's staff rapped once more

33

and a plinth bearing a golden Circlet rose from the dais. 'Then I invest you Lord President of the High Council. I wish you good fortune and strength.'

Gold Usher lifted the Circlet and holding it high moved over to the Doctor. 'I give you ... the Matrix,' he said solemnly, and placed the Circlet on the Doctor's head.

The Doctor stood there for a moment, the focus of the entire enormous assembly.

Then his face twisted and his body convulsed. His mouth opened in a kind of silent scream, as he tried frantically to claw the Circlet from his temples ...

# 4

## The Fugitive

For a moment no one moved, as the Doctor writhed in agony before them.

Then Leela sprang onto the dais, and hurled herself at the Doctor, knocking him from his feet. The Doctor fell headlong, and the force of his fall dislodged the Circlet from his brow. His body arched in a final spasm, and he slumped back unconscious.

'Doctor!' screamed Leela. A guard pulled her away.

'The Matrix rejects the candidate,' shouted Borusa triumphantly. 'Guards, seize him!'

Andred hesitated for a moment, then led his men forward. Gold Usher barred their way. 'Stop! None may lay hands on the president!'

'The Matrix has rejected him!' repeated Borusa.

'He *is* the Matrix now. It cannot reject him.' And with slight panic in his voice he cried, 'Surgeon General!'

Gomer hurried forward and knelt to examine the Doctor.

'Will he be all right?' asked Leela.

The old man went on with his examination, and did not reply. Leela waited anxiously.

Borusa and Gold Usher were still locked in argument.

'Surely you can see that this changes everything,' insisted Borusa. 'For a candidate to be attacked by the Matrix ... it's unheard of.'

'There is no *candidate*, Chancellor-Elect Borusa.

35

There is only the President. The Circlet *is* the Matrix Terminal. It can only be worn by the President, therefore this *is* the President.'

Stiffly Gomer rose. 'Moreover, Borusa, if you continue to stand there arguing legal technicalities, we shall find ourselves going through this whole boring business again, in the very near future.' Gomer was no respecter of ceremonies, or of Chancellors either.

Leela realised the significance of Gomer's words. 'You mean the Doctor is going to die?'

'Very possibly. For the moment he has retreated.'

'The Doctor does not retreat,' said Leela fiercely. 'He is no coward.'

'The retreat is purely a mental one, a simple defence reaction brought about by a sudden and unexpected attack on his conscious mind.'

'You see?' said Borusa triumphantly. 'There was an attack.'

'Oh have the kindness to be quiet, Borusa,' snapped Gomer. 'The President needs both rest and skilled medical attention. I shall supervise his case myself. We need a place of absolute security—and quiet.'

'May I be permitted to suggest the Chancellery?'

'The Chancellery will be perfect,' agreed Gomer. 'Take him away.'

Guards lifted the Doctor and carried him reverently from the Panopticon. Gomer turned to the Cardinal. 'As for you, Borusa, I suggest you cut off all communication with the President, prohibit all visitors, and keep your tedious bureaucratic problems to yourself.'

He hobbled off after the Doctor.

'Impertinence!' fumed Borusa. He was more used to delivering rebukes than to receiving them.

Kelner said soothingly. 'The Surgeon-General may

36

be a little impetuous, but I'm sure his hearts are in the right places!'

(In their war room the Vardans were conferring agitatedly. 'We are close,' whispered one of the council. 'So very close!'

The War Leader said, 'It is still too soon. He has little strength.'

One of the council said, 'Should he die, it will take a long time to replace him.'

'Too long. We must gamble upon his survival. Signal all Commanders to increase speed. We shall implement plan three.')

The murmuring was louder now, and the crowd around the dais thickened as Time Lords pressed forward to see what was going on. Borusa raised his voice. 'Time Lords! The President is unwell. We have taken him to the Chancellery. Remain calm. A bulletin will be issued shortly. Please leave the Panopticon quietly.'

As agitated Time Lords began filing out, he turned to Andred. 'Bring the girl, Commander. We must investigate her attack on the Doctor.'

'I didn't attack him,' protested Leela. 'I saved him.'

'The enquiry will determine that. Bring her!'

The Doctor lay stretched out on a couch in the Chancellor's office. Gomer was leaning over him, holding a tiny crystal phial to his neck. The colourless liquid flowed directly into the Doctor's blood stream. Gomer handed the empty phial to an assistant and straightened up.

37

'Well, Lord Gomer?' demanded Borusa impatiently.

'He has suffered a massive sub-mensan shock. I've given him a deranger dose but it will be hours perhaps days before he ...'

'Doctor!' said Leela delightedly. Everyone looked. The Doctor's eyes were open.

'Incredible,' murmured Gomer.

Leela hurried to the Doctor's side. 'Are you all right?'

'Quietly now,' warned Borusa.

The Doctor lifted his head. 'Ah Chancellor! What happened?'

'You suffered some kind of an attack,' said Borusa cautiously. 'In addition to which, your alien friend here knocked you down.'

'No, no, it was the Circlet,' insisted Leela. 'The Circlet was killing him!'

The Doctor sat up. He stared indignantly at Leela. 'What are you doing on Gallifrey?'

'You brought me.'

'Nonsense. It's forbidden to bring alien savages into the Capitol. Get rid of her.'

'Doctor, what's happened to you? It's me, Leela ...'

'Put her out, Commander,' ordered Borusa.

Andred took hold of Leela's arm. 'Out where, sir?'

'Outside the Capitol, of course.'

'In the outer world?' said Andred, shocked. The Capitol was so large that it covered most of Gallifrey. Indeed to a Time Lord, the Capitol was Gallifrey. The country outside was still surprisingly wild and primitive.

'That's right,' said the Doctor implacably. 'Expel her!'

'No,' said Leela desperately. 'Something's happened to your mind, Doctor, I won't leave you.'

'Take her!' ordered Borusa. The guards closed

38

in on Leela—but not soon enough.

She broke free of Andred's grip, dodged round him and made for the door. Two more guards moved to cut her off. She grabbed the nearest, threw him against his fellow, and flashed out of the door before the tangled guards could disentangle themselves.

'After her!' shouted Borusa.

The guards lumbered in pursuit. Leela was already disappearing down the corridor.

The leading guard drew his staser. 'Halt, or I fire!'

Leela went on running, weaving to and fro. The guard fired—and missed. Leela turned a corner and disappeared.

Andred came running up. 'Which way did she go?'

'She turned off down there, sir.'

'Well, don't just stand there—get after her!'

The guards ran off. Andred raised his wrist-communicator. 'This is Commander Andred. Sound the alarm, and turn out all available guards. An escaped alien prisoner is at large in the Capitol.'

A clangorous alarm bell began ringing through the corridors.

Leela sped through the long marble corridors, guards close behind her. She shot past two ancient Time Lords who were toddling along the corridor discussing the recent scandalous events in the Pan-opticon. The guards hurtled around the corner in pursuit. They raised their stasers. 'Stop, alien!' But the two old Time Lords blocked their view of Leela, and they couldn't get a clear shot.

By the time they had herded the astonished old men out of the way and taken up the pursuit, Leela had disappeared.


Andred came back into the Chancellor's office to find

39

the Doctor sitting up. 'That's funny, there's a ringing in my head.'

'I ordered the alarms to be sounded, sir. The girl got away.'

Kelner bustled in. 'What is happening? Who ordered those alarm——' he broke off at the sight of the Doctor. 'Your Excellency is feeling better?'

'Can't complain, Castellan,' said the Doctor cheerfully.

'Excellent—and now, Chancellor, if I may enquire...'

'The President ordered his female companion to be expelled from the Capitol. She got away.'

'I'll take charge of the operation myself, Your Excellency,' said Kelner.

'That's very brave of you. I warn you, Leela can be dangerous!'

'Have no fear Your Excellency, I shall see that she is driven out. Come, Commander.'

As Kelner departed the Doctor said plaintively. 'I wish someone would switch off that awful ringing in my head.'

Andred snapped an order and the sound died away.

'Ah, that's better,' said the Doctor.

Andred bowed, and followed Kelner leaving the Doctor and Borusa alone.

The old man looked down at his former pupil. 'What exactly are you playing at, Doctor?'

The Doctor grinned impudently up at him. 'A little more respect, if you don't mind. After all, I am President!'

'I thought respect was a quality you didn't admire, Doctor.'

'Ah, but that was before. I'd have thought you, of all people, would know me better, Chancellor.'

'You could never succeed in deceiving me when

you were a student at the Academy. You haven't changed in that respect—and neither have I. But this is rather more than a student prank—isn't it?'

'Believe me, Lord Borusa, I've never been more serious in my life—in any of my lives. While Leela remains free in the Capitol, we're all in danger.'

'Isn't that a little melodramatic—even for you?'

The Doctor yawned ostentatiously. 'Forgive me, my ordeal at the induction seems to have made me rather tired.'

Borusa bowed ironically. 'Then you must rest, My Lord President.'

'Thank you, my dear Chancellor-Elect.'

Borusa went to the door. 'We can continue our discussion when you have had time to rest—and when your alien friend has been captured and expelled. Meanwhile, I shall make sure that you are not disturbed.'

Borusa went out, and the Doctor heard his voice giving orders in the corridor outside. He waited for a moment, got up, and then tip-toed cautiously to the door, opening it a crack. He peered out into the corridor. Two guards were posted outside the room.

To keep others out, or to keep him in, wondered the Doctor. He could order them to go away—but would they obey him? Better not risk direct confrontation. His new and exalted position was far from secure.

The Doctor began pacing about the room. There was a tapestry on the wall behind Borusa's desk. The Doctor lifted it gently. It concealed a door.

'Can't fool me, Borusa, I knew you'd have a bolt-hole. Well done, Doctor!' He tried to open the door. It was locked. The Doctor felt in his pockets for his sonic screwdriver, and realised that he hadn't got any pockets—he was still in his induction robe.

He looked round the room, and saw his own clothes in the corner, arranged on a stand. He hurried over

41

to them ... The guards outside the Chancellor's office crashed to attention, as Andred came along the corridor. He tried to enter the room, but the guards Presented their stasers, barring his way. Andred glared at them. 'Out of my way. I want to see the president.'

'Sorry, sir. No one to enter. Chancellor Borusa's orders. No exceptions.'

Andred decided to save face as best he could. 'You know how to obey orders, I see. Good men!' He went on his way.


The Doctor completed dressing, winding his scarf around his neck and jamming his hat on the back of his head. He produced his sonic screwdriver and attacked the lock. Nothing happened. He tried again. Still nothing. He searched Borusa's desk, finding not a key but a map, which he promptly pocketed. 'Even the sonic screwdriver won't get me out of this one,' thought the Doctor and looked thoughtfully at the Chancellor's empty chair, addressing it as though Borusa still sat there. 'Now listen, I've got a problem. There's absolutely no point in having another door to your room if you haven't got a key. Well, is there? QED *Quod Erat Demonstrandum*. That's Latin. Latin and logic. But an actual key can be lost or stolen, therefore you're the key, Borusa. Palm print? No, that's too simple. Retina pattern?' He glared hard at the empty chair. 'No ... But you've got to admit, that you're very fond of the sound of your own voice.' He turned to the door. 'Open Sesame! I command you to open!' Nothing happened.

'Retina print, palm print, voice print ...' He looked accusingly at the chair. 'But you don't like voice prints, do you? You always used to say there's nothing more useless than a lock with a voice print!'

42

There was a whirr and a clunk from the door.

The Doctor spoke again, managing to produce a very creditable imitation of Borusa's acid tones. 'There's nothing more useless than a lock with a voice print!' The door swung open. Behind it was a short, dark passage.

The Doctor went down it, opened the door at the other end and emerged into the anteroom to the President's office.

Pausing a moment to get his bearings, he hurried off in the direction of the TARDIS.

Leela was trying to reach the TARDIS herself, but she'd been forced to hide in an alcove by the sudden appearance of a squad of guards.

Once they'd passed by, she emerged—and heard somebody coming down the corridor. She ducked back into cover. Somebody passed by.

Leela thought there was something very familiar about those footsteps. She popped her head out, and was just in time to see the Doctor disappearing round a corner.

Stealthily Leela moved after him.

Andred was in the Castellan's office, punching up shot after shot on the Capitol's video system. There were so many corridors, passages, antechambers and walkaways in the enormous old building that the chances of hitting the right one at the right time were very small, but Andred carried on trying, checking corridor after corridor in a random search pattern. Much to his own surprise, he came upon two furtive figures hurrying down a corridor. He looked up and called, 'Sir, I think I've found the alien.'

Kelner hurried over. 'Where is she?'

'There, sir. She's with the President.'

Kelner was outraged. '*With* the President?'

'Well, following him, anyway, sir. Line two, zero, two, sir.'

Kelner punched the controls on his desk monitor, and saw the Doctor striding swiftly down a corridor, Leela some little distance behind him.

Kelner switched on a communication circuit. 'Chancellor, this is Castellan Kelner. Is the President with you, by any chance? Still resting and not to be disturbed? I see ... Would you kindly inform me when he awakens? Thank you so much.'

Kelner looked up at Andred. 'Well, don't just stand there, Commander. Get after her!'

The Doctor had almost reached his destination when a squad of guards came marching round the corner, heading straight towards him. The Doctor made no attempt to run. As the guards came level with him he flipped open his coat. 'Bow to the Sash of Rassilon!' The guards bowed their heads in reverence at the sight of the gleaming metal sash, and the Doctor walked straight past them. The guards raised their heads to find their new President disappearing down the corridor, and a skin-clad alien figure hurrying towards them.

Leela pointed towards the Doctor. 'I'm with him,' she said, and before the astonished guards could react, she had slipped past them and was following the Doctor.

The Doctor hurried down the staircase that led to the antechamber, delighted to find the TARDIS still standing at the bottom. He sensed movement behind him, glanced over his shoulder, and caught a quick

44

glimpse of Leela ducking back into cover. Quickly, he opened the TARDIS door and went inside.

Meanwhile Andred had arrived and was interrogating his guards. 'Well, where is she?'

'She came this way, sir, but she was with the President——'

'Probably heading for the capsule,' muttered Andred. 'Come on!'

Leela ran up to the TARDIS door. It was closed against her. She began hammering on the door with her fists.

Inside the TARDIS, the Doctor stood silently, waiting. He made no attempt to open the door.

K9 was at the Doctor's feet. They could see Leela's face on the scanner, hear her anguished voice as she pounded on the door. 'Doctor, please, open the door! Please, let me in!'

The Doctor didn't move.

Beside him K9's head drooped sadly.

Andred and the guards hurried towards the TARDIS.

# 5

## The Betrayal

Leela heard a clatter of booted feet, abandoned her attempt to get inside the TARDIS, ducked round the back of it, and sped silently away.

Andred and his guards ran in from the other side and rushed up to the TARDIS. A guard tried unsuccessfully to open the door. 'It's locked, sir.'

'She must be in there. If the President's in there too she may try to harm him again.' Andred studied the TARDIS door. 'These old type forties have got some kind of trionic locking device. We'll need a set of cypher ident keys. Get moving, man!'

The guard hurried away.

The Doctor said, 'Well, K9, what d'you think? How are we doing so far?'

'Too many variables for accurate forecast.'

'What variables?'

'Illogicality of humanoid procedures.'

The Doctor grinned ruefully. 'Like me, you mean?'

'Affirmative, Master!'

'All right, then. How am I?'

The Doctor stood still, while K9 scanned him with his scissors.

'Cerebral circuits in functional order. Physical condition—dubious.'

'Thank you very much!'

K9 wasn't programmed for irony. 'Risks taken

46

appear to have been justified by results.'

'What are our chances if we proceed?'

'Actions so far indicate a success probability of thirty-nine point seven five.'

'That bad, eh?' said the Doctor thoughtfully. 'Are you sure?'

'Affirmative.'

The Doctor produced the map from Borusa's desk. 'Listen, I've discovered the location of the security control room—directly under the Panopticon, level three zero.'

K9 whirred and clicked. 'Success probability increased to forty-eight point three five.'

'That's better, eh? Not bad odds at all.'

'Any plan incorporating success factor below six five point zero is not advisable,' said K9 primly.

The Doctor began pacing to and fro. 'Suppose I can throw a mirror cast? A shadow shift to create a false image for space traffic control?'

'The plan is feasible. I suggest you proceed as follows——'

The Doctor held up his hand. 'Can I finish, please? I shall reflect the transmission beam off the security shield, feed it back through a linked crystal bank and boost it through the transducer.'

'I could not have given a better formulation of the plan myself, Master.'

'No, I don't think you could!'

'Possibility of your formulation being better than mine less than one per cent, however,' said K9 smugly.

'You really are the most insufferably arrogant, overbearing ...'

The Doctor broke off, smiling in spite of himself. 'You know, someone once said something very like that about me!'

'Correction Master. *Many* people have said some-

47

thing like that about you.'

'At least no one's ever called me smug!'

'Correction, Master. Many people have——'

'That will do, K9! Now listen ... if you destroy Security Control after I feed in the doppler effect and eliminate the Red Shift then surely the Invasion must succeed?'

'Probability of invasion success under conditions described rise to ninety-eight point two.'

The Doctor beamed. 'Well, what's a couple of points between friends?' He went to the TARDIS console and set to work.

Leela ran on and on through endless corridors, across bridges and walkways, through cloisters and anterooms until at last she found herself in a corridor that ended in a big arched doorway.

Cautiously, she moved through it and found herself in a small domed chamber. It held a control console, a set of monitor screens and an attractive, but bored young woman in Time Lord dress.

Without looking up the young woman said calmly. 'Come in!'

Leela crept forward drawing her knife. 'Where are your guards?' she whispered fiercely.

'I don't need any.'

Leela stepped swiftly forward and rebounded from an invisible barrier.

The young woman smiled. 'There's a forcefield between you and me. Between me and everybody, come to that. This is one of the highest security rated rooms in the entire Capitol.' She looked up at Leela. 'You must be that alien everyone's looking for. Leela isn't it? My name's Rodan. Put that ridiculous knife away before you hurt yourself.'

48

Leela sheathed the knife. 'The Doctor is always telling me to do that! Why do you not tell them I am here?'

'Why bother. That's their affair.'

'Whose affair?'

'The guards, the Time Lords, all the other boring people.'

She waved at the console and the monitors. 'Do you realise I've passed the Seventh Grade? Yet here I am, nothing more than a glorified traffic guard?'

'You are a guard?' Instinctively Leela drew her knife again.

'Oh do stop cavorting about like that, it's so undignified.'

Baffled and angry, Leela sheathed the knife again.

There was a buzzing from the instrument console. 'Oh, not again,' said Rodan wearily. 'Excuse me.' She touched controls and one of the monitors lit up. It showed a series of brightly coloured dots moving across a dark background. Rodan spoke into a communications unit in the same bored voice. 'Traffic control here. Yes, I have them on tracking. Clearance authorised.' She switched off the communicator. 'Primitive space fleet, neo-crystalline structure, atomic power and weaponry. On its way to blast some planet into dust, I suppose.'

'Then you must stop them.'

Rodan was horrified. 'What? That would be against every law of Gallifrey. We never interfere, you know, only observe.'

'What if they were to attack you?'

'Then they would be very stupid. Nothing—nothing —can get past the transduction barrier.' She yawned. 'Personally I find astrophysics a huge bore, don't you?'

Leela nodded dumbly.

49

Rodan said, 'Oh good, I knew I'd like you! Why don't you come in?' She touched a control, the invisible barrier vanished, and Leela fell into the room.

The Doctor looked up from the TARDIS console. 'K9, it's time for you to go and destroy the transduction barrier. Give me a few minutes to get away, and then set off.'

'Affirmative.'

'Good luck, K9,' said the Doctor softly. He opened the TARDIS door.

Andred and his guards were still grouped round the TARDIS awaiting the arrival of the keys. 'It seems to be fixed in this ridiculous shape,' said Andred amusedly. 'I wonder what it was imitating when it got stuck.'

The door opened and the Doctor appeared. Andred and the guards came to attention. 'My Lord President!'

The Doctor gave a start. 'Jelly babies,' he said mysteriously.

'I beg your pardon, sir?'

'I'd left my jelly babies in the TARDIS.' The Doctor produced a crumpled paper bag. 'Try one!'

Andred took one of the sweets and popped it cautiously in his mouth.

The Doctor said encouragingly. 'They're a delicacy I discovered on the planet Earth . . .'

Andred said indistinctly. 'That's Sol Three in Mutter's Spiral, isn't it, sir?'

'Well done, quite right. Do you like the jelly baby?'

'Delicious, sir.'

The Doctor pressed a sweet into his hand. 'Have another! Anybody who likes jelly babies can't be all bad.' He lowered his voice confidentially. 'You won't mention our meeting to the Chancellor, will you?

I don't think he appreciates jelly babies, he's got a frivolous mind.'

Andred was baffled but loyal. 'If that is what you wish, sir, I shall say nothing.'

'Good! Now—have you caught the girl yet?'

'No sir. We thought she might be in your capsule.'

'No, no,' said the Doctor airily, there's no one else in there.' He took Andred's arm, leading him away from the TARDIS. 'It's absolutely vital that she's caught and expelled from the Capitol. Absolutely vital!'

'Vital, sir,' repeated Andred. 'I'll see to it sir. Guards, follow me!'


For a moment the TARDIS stood there alone. Then Andred's guard bustled up carrying a flat box of cypher indent keys. He was surprised to find that everyone had gone, and even more surprised to find that the TARDIS door was now ajar.

Cautiously, he pushed it open and went inside.

Since he was a Time Lord guard, he was not surprised at the spacious control room within. What did surprise him was the dog-like metal automaton that peered curiously up at him.

Dropping the box of keys, he reached for his staser pistol.

K9 set his blaster on stun and shot the guard down. He glided past the man's unconscious body and out of the TARDIS.


Kelner tapped lightly on the door of the President's office and pushed it open. Borusa sat behind the President's desk. Trying it out for size no doubt, thought Kelner, who had ambitions in that direction

51

himself. His face a mask of polite concern Kelner said, 'My apologies, Chancellor. I take it the President is still resting in your chambers?'

The hawk-faced old man looked up at him. 'He is.'

'He has been there all the time?'

'He has. And I have been here.'

'I think you should rouse him now,' said Kelner delicately. 'I should very much like to speak to him ...'

Borusa looked thoughtfully at him for a moment, then rose and headed for the door. Politely Kelner moved aside to let him pass.


As the Doctor came back through the secret passage, there was a rapping on the outer door.

He heard Borusa's voice. 'Your Excellency, Castellan Kelner wishes to speak to you.'

The Doctor dashed to the couch and flung himself down. In a sleepy voice he called, 'What? Oh, very well, bring him in.'

Borusa and Kelner came into the room.

Kelner said obsequiously. 'I trust Your Excellency is rested?'

The Doctor nodded, and Kelner went on, 'I'm afraid I must tell you that the girl Leela has evaded our guards and is still in hiding somewhere in the Capitol.'

The Doctor rose angrily. 'How did this happen?'

'A regrettable oversight on the part of the guards.'

'She must be found,' shouted the Doctor. 'You are responsible for security, Castellan. See to it! Immediately!'

'Immediately, Your Excellency,' said Kelner, and scuttled away.

The Doctor said curtly, 'Borusa, call a meeting of my Council at once.'

'May I enquire——?'

'No!' said the Doctor rudely. 'You may not. Summon the meeting, immediately. No excuses!'

(Sleek, immense, shark-like, the Vardan flag-ship sped towards Gallifrey.)

Lights began flashing madly on Rodan's console, and she stared incredulously at the instrument readings. 'It can't be ... no one would dare.' She flicked the communicator switch. 'Space traffic control here. An alien space craft, two spans distance course zeroed in to Gallifrey. Raise transduction barrier to factor five. Repeat factor five. Immediate and urgent. Red Alert, repeat Red Alert!'

The stunned body of a technician lay sprawled across the doorway of the transduction barrier control room.

K9 glided past and regarded the massive equipment banks in front of him. Immense, automated incredibly powerful, the machinery in this room controlled the colossal forces that had kept Gallifrey safe from all invasion—until now.

Setting his blaster to maximum, K9 opened fire. Laser beams crackled, electrical panels sparked and burnt out, complex transduction circuitry melted and fused ... Soon the room was filled with smoke and flame.

Rodan was shouting into her communicator. 'Find him. I must find the Castellan! The transduction barrier has failed. Gallifrey is being invaded!' Rodan broke off as if unable to believe the horror of her own words.

Kelner entered the Panopticon conference hall to find the rest of the High Council already assembled. The Doctor lounged in his place at the head of the table. Kelner bowed low and took his place with the others.

The Doctor rose, looking mockingly around the set faces. 'My apologies for the haste, gentlemen, but this is no ordinary Council meeting. Today I am privileged to introduce you to your new masters.'

Three shimmering shapes began materialising in front of the conference table.

The Doctor threw back his head and let out a howl of maniacal laughter.

# 6

## The Invasion

The strange thing about the Vardans was that they weren't quite *there*. It was as if they existed in some other dimension, some other reality. The astonished High Council saw three tall, shimmering shapes, cloaked and hooded figures with the vaguest hint of features under the hoods. But somehow it was impossible to get a really good look at the Vardans. Something about them turned away the eyes.

At first, Borusa was more concerned with the improper behaviour of the Doctor than with the invading aliens. 'He is mad, I knew it!' Then he turned his attention to the invaders. 'Guards, destroy them!'

The nearest guard levelled his staser at the invaders. There was a flash of light from one of the shining shapes and the guard fell dead. It was as simple and horrible as that.

'Resistance is useless. Tell them, Doctor.' The voice was harsh and thin, and had something of the eerily unreal quality of the Vardans themselves. They were like ghosts, thought Borusa dazedly. Gallifrey was being invaded by shining ghosts!

'Resistance is useless,' repeated the Doctor obediently. 'The Vardans have more power than you have ever dreamed of, more knowledge than you could ever hope for. You must submit, as I did when I first made contact with them.'

'And when was that?' demanded Borusa.

'A long time ago,' said the Doctor wearily. 'I re-

55

ceived a telepathic message from the Matrix, warning me of their power, I decided to join them.'

Borusa gestured towards the shapes. 'You knew of this all the time—before your induction?'

'Even before that.'

'You disappoint me Doctor. I expected more of you.'

'Did you really? Thank you, Chancellor.' The Doctor turned to address the High Council. 'You will disperse and await my next commands. Inform the Capitol what has happened. There must be no resistance.'

Silently the Council began filing from the room. They seemed dazed, crushed—all except Borusa. 'You have no right to do this,' he said furiously.

'Borusa, have you carried out my orders?' said the Doctor suddenly.

'What orders—Supremacy?'

'Regarding the re-decoration of my office!'

'The matter was put in hand.'

'No doubt. But is it finished?'

'I believe so.'

'Make sure!' ordered the Doctor. 'Attend me there within the hour. I shall expect to see the work complete.'

Too angry to speak, Borusa turned away.

The Vardan Leader said, 'Congratulations, Doctor. You show great promise in the application of power. You could be a first-grade dictator.' This was quite a compliment. The entire Vardan philosophy was based on the seizure and application of power. A ruthless arbitrary dictator was the most admired figure in their society.

'Thank you,' said the Doctor humbly. 'That's very kind of you.'

'How long will it take you to find the Great Key?'

56

'That,' said the Doctor solemnly, 'is a matter of time.'

'The invaders are in control,' moaned Rodan.

Her world had suddenly crumbled around her, and she was in a state of near-hysterical collapse. Leela, on the other hand, was used to danger, and was positively exhilarated by it. Not surprisingly, it was Leela who took control.

'Good! Now they are here, we can fight them.'

'Didn't you hear the High Council's announcement. We must submit.'

'You listen to your High Council—I shall listen to my Doctor. He has a plan.'

'What plan?'

'I do not know.'

'Then how can you be so certain?'

'The Doctor always has a plan.' Rodan started to protest further, but Leela said, 'There is no point in further discussion. Talk is for the wise or the helpless, and I am neither.'

'What shall we do?'

'The Doctor wished me to be banished,' said Leela slowly. 'So, I will be banished!'

'Should we not surrender?'

'No!' said Leela fiercely. 'You talk always of surrender, of submission. Are all your tribe like this?'

'We are rational beings, we accept the situation.'

'You are cowards!' Leela went on thinking aloud. 'No, if the Doctor wished me banished, it was for a reason. I should have known that.'

'But the Doctor is a traitor!'

'Never!'

'But reason dictates——'

57

'Then reason is a liar.'

'But Leela, if I am right——'

'Then I am wrong, and I will face the consequences. Now, are you coming?'

Rodan nodded miserably. She switched off the force-field and followed Leela from the room.


The Doctor strode grandly into the Presidential office and found Borusa waiting. The place had been trans-formed. Walls, ceiling, doors, even the floor itself had been covered with intricately decorated lead panels. They were patterned in wheels and cogs and levers and they gleamed dully like the inside of some antiquated machine.

The Doctor looked round appreciatively. 'Nice, very nice indeed. A little too rococo for an aesthetic purist perhaps, but I like it.' He seemed to notice the Chancellor for the first time. 'Ah, Borusa! What are you doing here?'

'You wished to see me, Your Excellency.'

'I did? Now, what about ... Oh yes! Are the re-decorations to my office complete?'

'As Your Excellency can see ...'

'*Completely*, complete?'

'To the last detail.'

'No substitute materials, no forgeries, no penny-pinching?'

'No expense was spared,' said Borusa dryly. 'The materials and workmen were the finest to be had in the entire Thesaurian Empire.'

'Really?' said the Doctor admiringly. 'So *all* this exquisite relief work is in pure lead?'

Borusa decided that the combination of absolute power and knowledge of his own treason must have completely unhinged the Doctor's always erratic brain.

58

'Apart from a small admixture of strengthening alloy, that is the case.'

The Doctor smiled, and seemed to relax. Suddenly Borusa saw not a power-mad traitor, but the Doctor he had always known, the pupil whose impudent charm had so often brought an unwilling smile to his face.

The Doctor put an affectionate hand on the old man's shoulder. 'Good! Then at last we can really talk! Sit down.'

Borusa sat, and the Doctor began to speak. He talked for a very long while pouring out past history, information gained and future plans and Borusa listened in astonished silence.

When the Doctor had finished, Borusa shook his head in amazement. 'But why not simply warn us? Why the betrayal?'

'Would you have listened? The Time Lords had grown complacent, ripe for conquest. You needed the shock of invasion to wake up. Besides, once I had made contact with the Vardans, I had to pretend to join them to survive. Any attempt to warn you, and they'd have killed me, and invaded you just the same.'

'But to shield your feelings, your every thought for so long a time ... the strain must have been intolerable.'

'Difficult, I must confess, even for me. I owe you a great deal, Lord Borusa, and not least my apologies for all the indignities and insults I was forced to throw at you.'

'The President need apologise to no one.'

'Thank you.'

'The President need——'

'Thank no one either?' The Doctor smiled. 'True, very true, just a habit I picked up somewhere.'

By now Borusa had absorbed the problem, and was

59

considering how to deal with it. 'How accurate is your data?'

'Absolutely accurate, as far as it goes—but not yet complete.'

Borusa said thoughtfully, 'So, the Vardans can travel along wave-lengths of any sort. And since an electro-temporal field is needed for communications, they can read thoughts.'

'At almost any distance—*if* their attention is concentrated.'

Borusa looked around him. 'But a lead-lined room, such as this one ...'

'With at least a hint of elegance, I hope?' said the Doctor irrepressibly.

Borusa frowned at his old pupil's frivolity. 'A lead-lined room like this can shield us from them?'

'True.'

'And you managed at least partial shielding totally unaided?'

'Also true, but then, I had the benefit of your training!'

'Then why could I not shield myself?'

'Because, like the rest of the Time Lords, your mind is too logical. Most of you are lacking in humour, you have little imagination.'

Borusa gave an affronted sniff. Suddenly the Doctor said, 'What about tea?'

'Tea?'

'Tea!'

'Tea is the leaves of a plant, genus camellia in dried form.'

'I know what tea *is*—what's for tea?'

'What has tea got to do with the Vardan invasion?'

'Nothing! That's the whole point.'

'But I don't understand.'

'Of course you don't. You're too single minded.

60

Transparent as good old glass.'

'You're right,' said Borusa sadly. 'I wouldn't last a moment. My mind is too logical, too easy to read. The master learns from the pupil, eh, Doctor?'

'Well ...' said the Doctor modestly. But perhaps there was the faintest hint of smugness in his smile.

Rodan led Leela through the Capitol, looking for the little used tunnel that led to the outside. As they moved along, the corridors became narrower and more neglected-looking, almost disused. The Time Lords seldom ventured into the outside world.

Rodan paused at a corridor junction. 'Straight on, I think. Though I'm not really sure. I've never been this far.'

A voice behind them shouted, 'Halt!'

They turned, and saw Andred, covering them with a staser. 'Where do you two think you're going?'

'Outside,' said Leela briefly.

'Don't you know we've been invaded?'

'As a matter of fact, we do, Commander Andred,' said Rodan. 'I was on duty in space traffic control when it happened.'

She told Andred of the arrival of the alien craft, and of the mysterious failure of the transduction barrier. Andred in turn told them of the astonishing events on the council chamber, and of the Doctor's strange behaviour.

'Well,' said Rodan, when he'd finished. 'What are you going to do about all this?'

'I'm not sure yet. How much is this alien girl involved with the invaders.'

'I don't think she even knows who they are.'

'But she's the President's friend—and he is working for them.'

61

'He isn't, he's only pretending to help them,' said Leela fiercely.

'I see! So you and the Doctor only want to help us. I suppose that's why you destroyed the transduction barrier.'

'I destroyed nothing.'

'She couldn't have done it, Andred,' said Rodan. 'She was with me when it happened.'

'Someone blew up the control room. Who was it, if it wasn't her?'

'I've no idea. All we want is to get out of here.'

'Why?'

'Because it's too dangerous on the inside, and Leela thinks we may be able to do some good outside.'

Leela was getting impatient. Her hand hovered near the hilt of her knife, and she was poised to spring. She rather liked Andred, but she was quite prepared to kill him if he stood in her way. 'Well, are you going to let us go or not?'

Andred holstered his staser. 'All right. Carry on this way and you'll come to the exit tunnel. But be careful, there's a curfew. If any of the guards see you they'll shoot—Kelner's orders.'

'Why don't you come with us?'

'I can do more good here. Someone's got to keep an eye on Castellan Kelner and besides, there may be a chance of having a go at the invaders.' He gave Leela a look. 'Or even the president.'

Leela gave him an angry glare but said nothing. Andred scarcely knew the Doctor after all, and he couldn't be expected to share her own blind faith in him. 'Come on, Rodan,' she said, and led the way down the corridor.

Half-regretfully, Andred watched them go.

*

62

The Doctor and Borusa had nearly finished their discussion.

'By the way,' said Borusa as they prepared to leave, 'why did you order your friend Leela to be banished?'

'For her own protection. Leela is a barbarian, a primitive. She's quite incapable of shielding her feelings or emotions.'

Borusa nodded. 'So, if I'm as transparent as good old glass . . .'

'Leela is even more so. She's a danger to herself and to us all. But once she gets outside . . .'

'That barbarian garden? How will she be safer there?'

'Because that barbarian garden is her natural habitat. She's a huntress, a creature of instinct. There's no power out there, no technology to confuse her . . .'

Borusa shuddered. It was beyond his comprehension that anyone could live without civilisation. 'How awful! Will she be able to survive?'

'I don't know.' The Doctor got to his feet. 'We'd better go and face them, Chancellor. They'll get suspicious if we stay out of sight too long.'

Borusa got stiffly to his feet. 'You haven't told me very much about your plans.'

'As much as I dare,' said the Doctor apologetically.

'Quite so. The less I know, the less I can give away.'

'You must block from your mind the little that I have told you,' warned the Doctor. 'Can you do it? Can you act as you did before?'

'Yes!' said Borusa determinedly.

'Well done,' said the Doctor gently. 'You're a very brave man, Cardinal Borusa.'

63

# 7

## The Outcasts

By now Leela and Rodan were outside the Capitol, making their way across a bleak and windswept stretch of moorland.

The journey through the outer corridors had brought them to a narrow tunnel, which ended in a kind of airlock, a precaution against the possibility of the natural atmosphere contaminating the air-conditioned calm of the Capitol. Rodan had operated controls, they had gone through a narrow door, that led Outside. The door slid closed behind them, and suddenly they were in open country, the sheer white walls of the Capitol rising incredibly high above them.

The change in conditions had affected the two girls in completely different ways. Leela was cheerful, exhilarated, delighted to feel wind with a hint of rain in her face, springy turf underfoot instead of cold, hard marble.

Rodan was soon feeling cold and frightened. Deprived of the comforting warmth of the Capitol she was lost, helpless. 'Leela, I must rest. I'm so tired.'

Leela glanced over her shoulder. Although they had been crossing the moor for quite some time, the gleaming towers of the Capitol were still in sight. 'No, we have not come far enough yet.'

Rolling moorland stretched endlessly ahead, rising and falling, broken only by occasional clumps of trees.

'I never thought Outside would be like this,' sobbed Rodan. 'It's so empty.'

'Surely you have been outside before?'

'Never. None of us come Outside. Why should we? Everything we need is in the Capitol.'

'Here is better,' said Leela confidently.

'But it frightens me.'

'You are frightened? Why?'

'It's all so—empty.'

'We must go on,' said Leela firmly. 'We can still see the city, so those in the city can see *us*.'

'How much further?'

'To the other side of the hill. Then we can rest.'

Leela began striding light-footed across the turf. With a reproachful look, Rodan stumbled after her.

It seemed to take forever to climb the hill and descend the other side, but they managed it at last, and Rodan threw herself down, close to the edge of a little wood.

'Now can we rest?'

'Yes, for a while.'

Rodan dropped to the ground in a heap. Leela looked round carefully, and sat beside her.

Rodan took off her flimsy sandals and rubbed her sore feet. 'Why did I listen to you. It was stupid to leave the Capitol.'

'Would you rather stay with the invaders? At least we're safe out here.'

An arrow flashed through the air and stuck quivering in the ground just in front of them.

Rodan jumped to her feet with a scream. Leela was on her feet, her knife in her hand. 'Quickly, Rodan, run!'

But it was too late. Men with spears ran out from

the trees, and gathered around them in a menacing circle. They were trapped.

Castellan Kelner regarded the hulking guard standing rigidly to attention before him. The guard's name was Varn. He was very big, very brave, and very stupid. Best of all, he was utterly loyal to Castellan Kelner, who had recognised his qualities, and promoted him to the command of the Castellan's bodyguard, an elite squad who took orders only from Kelner. 'Now then, Varn, you understand your new appointment? From now on you will guard the President. You will stay with him at all times, is that clear?'

'Yes, Castellan.'

'You will report to me everything the President says or does.'

'Yes, Castellan.'

'The President has enemies, Varn, and there may be those who wish to harm him. You will protect him from any such attack—unless I order otherwise.'

'Yes, Castellan. Nothing will happen to the president while I am guarding him.'

'Good. You see, if anything did happen to the President I might have to take over as President myself. I have no desire to expose myself to the dangers of that position—for the moment, that is.'

'I understand, Castellan.'

'Good. You will take up your new position immediately. But remember, Varn, you are still serving me. When the time comes, I will see that you are suitably rewarded for your loyalty.'

'Yes, sir. And thank you, sir.'

Varn saluted and marched massively from the room.

Kelner smiled. He was not yet sure exactly where the Doctor stood, and until he was, it was difficult to

66

decide whether he wanted him alive or dead. Only time would tell. Meanwhile Varn would be at the Doctor's side. To protect, or to kill him—just as Kelner ordered.

In the centre of the woods there was a tiny clearing, and in the clearing was a long hut. It was made of un-peeled logs, roofed with turf and camouflaged with branches, and it blended almost perfectly into its surroundings. A man came out of the hut and stood waiting before the door as a group of men with spears dragged two female captives into the clearing. The man was called Nesbin, and he was the leader of the strange community known as the Outsiders. Nesbin was tall and strong, roughly dressed with harsh, craggy features. He wore a kind of simple smock, and a headband kept shaggy shoulder-length brown hair from his eyes. He and his followers had the weatherbeaten look of people who lead hard lives in the open air.

Thoughtfully Nesbin studied the two captives. One was a Time Lady of the kind he had often seen before, though she had none of the usual elegance of her kind. Her face was dirty, her robes tattered and she looked tired and frightened.

The other captive was more of a puzzle, a tall skin-clad girl with reddish-brown hair. She was struggling furiously with the two men who held her arms.

Nesbin's men were almost as bedraggled as their captives. Most seemed to be bruised, and one or two had roughly-bound wounds.

Nesbin stared at Ablif, a burly young man who was the leader of the hunting party.

'What's this, Ablif? Have you been in a battle?'

Ablif rubbed at a deep scratch on his brown cheek. 'We found these two hiding on the edge of the forest.'

67

'Were they armed?'

Ablif nodded towards the girl in skins. 'This one was. Took the whole lot of us to get this off her.' He tapped a long bladed knife thrust into his belt.

At a nod from Nesbin, the two men holding Leela dragged her closer. He studied her thoughtfully. 'She's a strange one all right.' He reached out and touched her hair.

Immediately a foot lashed out, kicking his right leg from under him. 'Keep your hands off me!' hissed a furious voice.

Nesbin got slowly to his feet, trying to ignore the grins on the faces of his men. 'Well, well, it speaks!'

'I am not an "it". I am Leela, and this is Rodan. Who are you, and what do you want from us?'

'My name is Nesbin. I am leader here. More to the point, what do you want with us?'

Rodan spoke for the first time. 'We don't want anything with you.'

A tall bony woman called Presta came out of the log hut. 'It's a trick. She's a Time Lady, isn't she? Send her back to the Capitol where she belongs.'

Rodan was horrified. 'No, you mustn't do that—we're escaping from the Capitol.'

'Escaping? What for?'

Briefly Rodan told him of the Vardan invasion.

Nesbin took the news calmly, almost as if it didn't much concern him. 'So, you do want something from us then. Food, protection, help. You can't survive out here on your own.'

'I can survive anywhere!' said Leela fiercely.

'That I can believe. What are you anyway, girl? You're not from Gallifrey, are you?'

'I am a warrior of the Sevateem.'

'She's an alien,' said Presta worriedly. 'Aliens are forbidden on Gallifrey. It's dangerous to keep her

68

here, the guards will surely come hunting for her.'

'We'll think about that in a moment,' said Nesbin. He looked hard at Leela. 'Well, *warrior*, perhaps you might survive. What about your friend here? I doubt if she's ever set foot outside the Capitol before.' He turned to Rodan. 'Well have you?'

'No,' muttered Rodan.

'It's all different out here, you know, you have to fend for yourself. How are you going to eat?'

Rodan produced a handful of tablets from the pouch at her belt. 'I have supplies.'

'They won't last long. How will you manage when they're finished? Have you ever eaten flesh, or fruit? Do you know how to find shelter? You wouldn't last three days out here!'

Nesbin seemed to be taking a positive pleasure in taunting Rodan; he obviously had some grudge against Time Lords. By now Rodan was near to tears. 'I didn't realise. Oh, I'm so tired, and cold ...'

Nesbin said gruffly, 'All right, all right ... You'd better get inside.'

'Are you going to let them stay then?' demanded Presta.

'We'll decide when we've heard more about this invasion.'


K9 glided through the corridors of the Capitol like some great metal rat, keeping close to the walls, hiding in quiet corners, behind statues and tapestries, lurking in patches of shadow. Several times he narrowly escaped being seen by patrols of guards, and once three shimmering alien shapes glided along a nearby corridor, making K9's antennae bristle with their alien presence.

At last K9 reached his goal. Swiftly he glided up to

69

the still-open door of the TARDIS and disappeared inside.

Once inside the control room, K9 paused and gave out a complex series of beeps. Activated by remote control, the door slid closed behind him.

More bleeps, and a small panel slid open in the base of the control console. K9 glided up to it and extended his main antenna so that it fitted into the socket inside the panel. The TARDIS console hummed into life. K9's eye-screens lit up and all his antennae quivered ecstatically, as data began flooding in from the TARDIS console.

The next stage of the Doctor's plan was under way.

The Doctor swept into Kelner's office, followed by Borusa. The Cardinal's face was grim. The Doctor however was in high good humour.

Kelner was not alone in his opulent office. Two tall, hooded shapes were shimmering at his side.

'I'm sorry to have kept you waiting,' said the Doctor cheerfully.

Kelner bowed his head. 'Not at all, Your Excellency.'

'I wasn't talking to you,' said the Doctor, with a nod to the Vardans. He installed himself behind Kelner's desk. 'Right, shall we start? These are your new masters, and I authorise you both to acknowledge their absolute power.'

'I am Acting-Chancellor,' said Borusa stiffly. 'You have no authority under the Constitution to order me to do any such thing.'

'The Constitution is suspended,' said the Doctor. 'As of now!'

'This is monstrous.'

'Yes, but it's happening Borusa, so just do as you're told!'

70

'Never. I will not submit to these aliens. I am a Time Lord, a Cardinal——'

A ray of light shot from one of the shimmering shapes, a red glow suffused Borusa's frail old body, and he twisted and fell.

# 8

## The Assassin

Even in his agony, Borusa managed to mutter defiance. 'I will not submit ... I will not submit ...'

The red glow burned more fiercely.

'Stop,' shouted the Doctor. 'Don't destroy him. He can still be useful to us.'

'You will be responsible for him?' said the Vardan threateningly.

'Yes.'

The glow faded and Borusa lay still. The Doctor looked down at him. 'He can't help being so stiff-necked. Castellan, have the Chancellor removed to his quarters. Don't let anyone in or out, he's under house arrest.'

Kelner was terrified. 'Immediately, sir. Guards, you heard the President.'

Two guards came forward and helped Borusa to his feet. The old man was recovering fast, though still very weak. Sustained only by his indomitable will, he shook off the aid of the guards and walked from the room.

The Doctor looked after him. 'You have to admire him, you know, he does have courage.'

'He is a fool,' said the Vardan dispassionately. 'If he causes trouble we shall destroy him—and you also.'

The Doctor looked hurt. 'I've kept my part of the bargain so far, haven't I? What more do you want?'

'More?' The Vardan's voice was scornful. 'We have not begun yet, Doctor. When we are certain that we have achieved complete dominance over your people, we will reveal our requirements to you.'

'And return to your true forms? I find it disconcerting, talking to shimmering shapes.'

'The time is not yet right. First, you must complete the arrangements for the conquest of your people.'

'Naturally, naturally,' said the Doctor, as if this was a matter of only minor importance. 'Well, Castellan, the Chancellor doesn't seem too keen to help us. What about you?'

Wringing his hands in terror, Kelner bowed low. 'It is my duty to serve the President at all times. My only desire is to do whatever you wish.'

'Somehow I thought you'd see things like that. You can start by making sure nobody tries to organise any sort of resistance. That's the last thing we want.'

'Yes, sir, I quite agree. Peaceful co-operation is a much more fruitful course.'

'That's the idea. Listen, why don't you just regard yourself as acting Vice-President, eh?'

Kelner was thrilled. 'Thank you, sir.'

'You'd better make me a list of all Time Lords in official positions—the ones you think are reliable.'

'Yes, of course, sir.'

'And you'd better give me a list of known troublemakers as well,' added the Doctor carelessly. 'Just so we know who's most likely to resist.'

'Immediately, sir. I'll begin at once.'

'That's the stuff,' said the Doctor encouragingly. 'Off you go then.'

Kelner hurried away and the Doctor turned to the Vardans. 'I knew we'd be able to rely on him. Well, now you're safely here, why don't you relax, make yourselves at home?'

Sitting down, the Doctor swung his feet up on Kelner's desk and beamed at the two Vardan invaders as

73

if he hadn't a care in the world.

The Vardans shimmered and vanished.

The Doctor grinned. 'Unsociable lot!'

He sat there for some time, staring into space, thinking hard. He was still in the same position some time later, when Kelner hurried back into the room. 'Ah, there you are, Kelner!'

'Is there anything more I can do for you, sir?'

'Yes, get me a jelly baby.'

Kelner looked baffled and the Doctor said, 'In my right-hand pocket, man.'

Kelner hurried round the side of the chair. Gingerly, he fished the bag of jelly babies out of the Doctor's pocket.

'What colour would you prefer, sir?'

'Orange.'

'There doesn't seem to be an orange one left, sir,' said Kelner worriedly.

He offered the bag and the Doctor took a jelly baby at random. It was black. 'One grows tired of jelly babies, Kelner.'

'Indeed, one does, sir.'

'Tired of almost everything—except power.'

'Yes, sir.'

'Except power,' repeated the Doctor musingly. 'Is the curfew effective, Castellan?'

'Yes, sir. No incidents have been reported.'

'Splendid! What a superbly subservient Capitol you run, Castellan.'

'You are most generous, sir.'

The Doctor's voice hardened. 'Where are those lists I asked for?'

Kelner jumped, produced a mini-recorder and handed it to the Doctor.

The Doctor touched a control, and a list of names began flowing across the tiny screen. 'I see. These are

74

the people you feel we can rely on.' He adjusted the setting, and another list appeared. 'And these are the Time Lords you regard as potential rebels against our regime?'

'I do, sir. I've checked bio-data extracts of all the Time Lords in the Capitol personally.'

'Have you now?'

'With one or two exceptions,' added Kelner hastily. 'Such as your good self, of course.'

'I should think so too!' The Doctor frowned at the recorder. 'Well, if these are our potential rebels, we'd better do something about them, hadn't we?'

Suddenly a Vardan was with them. 'Unreliable elements must be destroyed.'

The Doctor beamed at the newcomer. 'Oh, I hardly think so. I'm sure they can be all made to see reason, given time. Besides, they have a good deal of knowledge and experience between them. Some of them might be very useful.'

'They must be destroyed. There is no other choice.'

'Oh, but there is, isn't there Kelner?'

Kelner had no wish to become involved in a dispute between the Doctor and his new masters. 'There is?'

'Expulsion!'

'Oh, yes, an excellent idea, sir.'

The Doctor looked at the Vardan. 'None of them can survive out there without help—and there *is* no help out there.'

Kelner hastened to agree. 'It really would be an admirable deterrent. All Time Lords fear the Outside. Once they realise that rebels face expulsion, they'll soon come to heel.'

The Vardan said, 'Very well. We approve. But Chancellor Borusa will be kept here in confinement as a hostage.'

'Naturally, naturally,' said the Doctor. 'All right,

75

Castellan, get on with it. I suggest you put them out one at a time—the effect will be more terrifying if they don't have company.'

'Yes, sir. I'll start immediately, sir.'

Kelner hurried away.

The Doctor beamed at the two Vardans. 'A good day's work, wouldn't you say?'

'Your progress so far has been—satisfactory,' said the Vardan grudgingly.

'Listen. Don't you think it's time you showed a little trust? You could relax now, materialise properly.'

'It is not yet time. Your next task is to dismantle the Quantum force field around Gallifrey.'

'I sabotaged the barriers so you could come through. But dismantling the force field completely—that's impossible.'

'You will find a way.'

'But if we tamper with the force field the whole planet may vaporise!'

*You will find a way!*

'I can't ...'

*You will.*' The Vardan disappeared. The discussion was ended.

Suddenly cheerful again, the Doctor snapped his fingers at his bodyguard Varn, who stood waiting by the door, and hurried from the room.

Varn hurried after him.


A fire burnt in the centre of the log hut, and the air was warm and smoky. Leela and Rodan sat in the middle of a circle of grim-faced Outsiders, while Nesbin questioned them in detail about the invasion of Gallifrey.

When he was satisfied he had extracted all they knew, Nesbin growled. 'Gallifrey invaded, eh? It was

76

supposed to be impossible.'

'How do you know that?' asked Leela. 'You're not Time Lords, are you?'

'Oh, but we are,' growled Nesbin. 'Some of us, anyway. Or at least, we were—until we decided to drop out.'

'Drop out? You fell from the Capitol?'

'Some of us were expelled, others left of their own accord. All that peace and tranquillity can get very boring, you know.'

Leela turned to Rodan. 'Does he speak the truth?'

'Sometimes rebels and criminals are punished by expulsion. I've heard rumours of people leaving voluntarily, but it's a subject that's never mentioned.'

'No, it wouldn't be,' said Nesbin scornfully. 'It might upset their cosy little world, where violence is taboo.'

(Nesbin himself had been expelled for physically attacking a rival Time Lord, an offence almost unknown in Time Lord society.)

'Then you are ready to fight,' said Leela. 'Good!'

'Now wait a minute girl——'

'No! You must listen to me, before it is too late. I tell you we must fight.'

'Why should we listen to you? You can't even look after yourselves.'

Ablif was sitting close to Leela, and before anyone could stop her she snatched her knife from his belt, and jumped to her feet. 'Try me!'

Leela was crouched cat-like, ready to spring. Suddenly Nesbin knew that not only was she capable of killing him, she was positively looking forward to it. He backed away. 'We'll settle this later, when I'm not so busy.'

Leela swung round on the Outsiders. 'Listen to me, all of you. Gallifrey is your planet, and it has been invaded. Whatever your differences with the Time

Lords, you must fight to defend it! Are we agreed?'

There was a fierce growl of agreement from the crowd.


Castellan Kelner was in the process of expelling Gomer, taking a good deal of pleasure in the task. 'Your record shows that you are politically unreliable, Lord Gomer.'

Standing before Kelner's desk, flanked by two guards, Gomer was quite unafraid. 'How dare you, Kelner. There isn't a more loyal Time Lord on Gallifrey.'

'Loyal to the old ways, perhaps.'

'What other ways are there?' asked Gomer simply. 'Honour does not change.'

Kelner scowled under the implied rebuke. 'We consider you to be dangerous, a threat to the new regime.'

'At my age, I take that to be a compliment, Castellan Kelner. I may be getting on, but if I knew of any way of attacking these invaders ...'

'You'd do it!' concluded Kelner. 'Yes, I'm sure you would. We'll all be safer with you out of the way.'

'What are you going to do with me?'

'By order of the president, you are to be expelled from the Capitol.'

To Gomer's ears it was a death sentence, but he accepted it unflinchingly. 'I go gladly. I prefer to die honourably, even Outside, than to live on here as a slave.'

Andred stepped forward. 'You'd better come with me, sir,' he said gently, and led the defiant old man away.

Execution of sentence was immediate, and soon Gomer was being marched along the corridors leading towards the Outside. The walk was a long one and the old man's steps began to falter. 'I'm sorry, I can't go any faster, it's my age, you know. I'm nearing the end of this regeneration.'

'Yes, sir, I know,' said Andred gently. 'You just set your own pace.'

'In my younger days I was considered lively enough,' said the old man sadly. 'I was quite a rebel.'

'No doubt that's why you're being expelled now, sir.'

'No doubt. Kelner and I never got on, you know, never saw eye to eye. To tell you the truth, I still can't stand the fellow.'

'You're not alone in that, sir.'

Gomer chuckled. 'You'd better take care, young fellow, or you'll be following me Outside.'

'I don't think so, sir. Some of us are going to try and change things.'

Gomer nodded warningly towards the two guards, and Andred smiled.

'Don't worry, sir, they're on our side. So are quite a few others, more than Kelner and the president realise. We're gaining new recruits all the time.'

Gomer was delighted. 'Good for you young fellow, good for you! Can I stay and help?'

'Thank you sir, but I'm afraid I must put you Outside, for the time being at least. We're not ready to attack yet, and Kelner will grow suspicious if the expulsions aren't carried out.'

'I understand.'

'But you may find help Outside, sir. The Outsiders may be rebels and criminals, but I'm sure they'll be loyal to Gallifrey. Rodan and the alien girl are out there already. Try to find them, I'm sure they'll help you if they can.'

Gomer nodded and hobbled bravely towards his fate.

79

They reached the tunnel to the Outside and then Andred led Gomer through it. He blenched at the sight of the bleak empty moor, but his courage did not fail him. 'Goodbye, young man, and good luck.'

'Good luck to you sir.'

For a moment Andred watched the frail old figure hobble across the moorland. Then, grim-faced, he turned and went back to the Capitol.

A short time later, in a hidden vault beneath the Panopticon, Andred was addressing a small meeting of rebel guards and Time Lords, telling them of Gomer's expulsion, and of more expulsions to follow. 'We must act soon,' he concluded, 'and the first thing we must do is kill the President!'

A shocked murmur of protest came from the little group.

'I know it's against every law of Gallifrey, and I know it will mean my breaking my sacred oath, but there is no other way. The new President has forfeited the right to our protection. He is the traitor who made this invasion possible, and he must die for it. Are you with me?'

There was a moment of silence. To a Time Lord an elected President had a sacred aura.

'Well?' said Andred fiercely.

'I agree,' said a guard grimly. 'I don't *like* it, but it's the only way.' There was a reluctant chorus of assent.

'Right. Well, first we must find him when he's away from his alien friends—and away from that tame bodyguard Kelner's given him. Then we can strike!'

The Doctor was trying very hard to get away from his tame bodyguard at that very moment. He had been marching the man up and down the Capitol on a

80

vague tour of inspection for ages, but Varn refused to be shaken off.

'May I ask where we're going now, sir?' he panted.

'Sssh!' said the Doctor mysteriously. 'I'm not at liberty to tell you.'

The Doctor led the way briskly down a few more corridors, then into a small ante room where a blue box stood at the bottom of a ramp. He produced a key, and opened the door of the box.

Varn started to follow him.

The Doctor halted. 'No, no, you stay outside.'

'I can't sir, I must stay with you. Castellan's orders.'

The Doctor was struck by a sudden inspiration. He flung open his coat to reveal a shining chain of linked bands across his chest. 'Do you know what that is?'

Varn bowed his head. 'Yes, Your Excellency. The Sash of Rassilon!'

'Then obey me.'

'The Castellan will have me shot, sir.'

'Don't worry,' said the Doctor cheerfully. 'If he does, I'll have *him* shot. Now, you stay there, I'll only be a moment. Tell you what, I'll leave the door open.'

Varn nodded reluctantly, and the Doctor slipped inside the TARDIS. He found K9 still plugged into the TARDIS console.

'How's it going K9?' There was no reply. 'K9?'

The Doctor realised that K9 was completely immersed in his greatest pleasure, the absorption of fresh data. He was in a kind of blissful electronic trance.


Varn was wondering whether it was his duty to follow the Doctor into the TARDIS when his doubts were temporarily put to rest by a staser-butt behind the ear. Andred caught the body and lowered it to the ground, helped by two of his guards. They had spotted

81

the Doctor on their way back from the secret meeting, and the opportunity had seemed too good to miss.

'I shall go in first,' whispered Andred. 'You two keep a lookout for any more of Kelner's bodyguards.'


'K9! K9! K9!' said the Doctor reprovingly. 'This is no time to enjoy yourself.' He grabbed K9's tail antenna and with an effort lugged him free of the console. The connection broken, K9 looked up at him reproachfully.

'Absorption of data was proceeding most satisfactorily, Master.'

'Here, take this,' said the Doctor. He took the Matrix Circlet from his pocket and put it on K9's head, adjusting it to connect with K9's antenna. Unbuckling the Sash he slipped it over K9's head so that Sash and Circlet formed a kind of unit.

K9's eyes lit up and all his antennae went rigid. 'Primary circuits locked in, commencing secondary feed.'

'Take it easy old chap,' warned the Doctor. Such a sudden and massive data in-put was a strain even for K9.

The Doctor heard movement behind him and turned.

Andred was looming over him, staser in hand.

'Andred, what a pleasant surprise! You're just in time, I've got something for you.'

Andred levelled his staser-pistol at the Doctor's head. 'In the name of liberty and honour, traitor, I sentence you to die!'

# 9

## The Vardans

The Doctor said, 'Please don't do that, I am the President, you know, show some respect, stun him, K9!'

K9 did. Andred slumped to the floor.

'Well, don't just stand there,' said the Doctor ungratefully. 'Get on with it, reconnect.'

'Commencing re-connection.' K9 resumed his communion with the Matrix.


The ominous shimmering presence of a Vardan at his elbow, Castellan Kelner sat studying his monitor screen. On it was a picture of a number of Andred's guards lurking furtively around the TARDIS. Kelner didn't quite understand what was going on, but he had seen more than enough to worry him. Nervously, he made a decision snapping his fingers to summon the bodyguard in the doorway. 'Take a squad and arrest Commander Andred and the guards who are with him. If they resist, kill them.'

The bodyguard saluted and departed.

'Something is wrong?' enquired the Vardan coldly.

'Nothing my bodyguard cannot deal with,' said Kelner hastily. 'Just an infringement of discipline to be punished.'

'You act correctly. Lack of discipline cannot be tolerated.'

Kelner looked pleased. He was going to get on well

with his new masters after all. Perhaps even better than the Doctor. In which case ... was the Doctor's continued existence really necessary?

'Come on, K9,' said the Doctor impatiently. 'Get on with it, they'll start to miss me soon.'

He was so absorbed that he failed to notice that Andred had recovered and was rising groggily to his feet, the staser still in his hand. 'Die, traitor!'

'Not now,' said the Doctor absently. 'Can't you see I'm busy?'

Andred fired.

Nothing happened.

He fired again and again, still with no result.

'It won't work in here,' explained the Doctor calmly, 'not inside the relative dimensional stabilizer field.'

'Then why did you tell that thing to stun me?'

'I wanted you out of the way for a bit. Now, are you going to behave, or shall I tell K9 to stun you again? I'd sooner not bother K9, he's rather busy.'

Andred holstered his useless staser. 'What treachery are you attempting now?'

'Something rather more efficient than your recent efforts I hope!'

The Doctor returned his attention to the console. 'Come on, K9, get on with it.'

The bodyguard squad marched swiftly up to the TARDIS, taking Andred's guards completely by surprise. There was a brief useless attempt at resistance, which ended in massacre as the bodyguard squad ruthlessly shot down Andred's men.

As the crackle of staser-bolts died away, the squad

84

leader raised his communicator. 'Operation completed, Castellan.'

'You might as well surrender, Doctor,' said Andred. 'This capsule is surrounded by my men. There's no way you can go outside and stay alive.'

The Doctor ignored him. 'K9, I'm going outside for a moment, I'm relying on you. Don't let this idiot touch anything.'

The Doctor headed for the door.

'Goodbye, Doctor,' said Andred ironically, and waited for the sound of staser fire.

The Doctor came out of the TARDIS and surveyed the bodyguard squad with a look of lordly surprise. 'What's going on here?'

'These men were trying to assassinate you, sir.'

'Did you have to kill them?'

'Yes,' said the bodyguard bluntly.

'Yes, I suppose you did.'

'My lord President, I don't think you realise the seriousness of the situation.'

'Oh yes I do! There's been an attempt on my life, and you've let the ringleader escape. Where's Commander Andred, eh? Not here, is he?'

The bodyguard looked down at the dead men. 'Don't worry, sir, he won't get far.'

'I should hope not! You'd better find him, before he comes back and has another go.'

The squad leader saluted and hurried off, followed by his men.

The Doctor went back inside the TARDIS. He smiled grimly at Andred's astonished face. 'No way I can go out there and live, eh Andred? I've got news for you, my friend. You're the one who's stuck here, your pitiful revolution has failed.'

'You're lying!'

'I wouldn't be alive if I was,' said the Doctor. 'What do they teach you chaps at the military academy, these days? If you can't pull off a simple palace revolution, what can you pull off?'

Andred hurried to the TARDIS door and tried to open it, but it was shut fast. 'It's jammed!'

'It's *locked*,' corrected the Doctor. 'It's going to stay locked until the invaders have gone. While I'm in here they can't touch me, and they can't read my thoughts, either.'

'What are you talking about? Read your thoughts?'

'Let me tell you a little about the Vardans,' said the Doctor wearily, and proceeded to do so.

'So they can travel along any form of broadcast wavelength?' said Andred. 'Send image projections of themselves, as they're doing now, or materialise completely if they want to?'

'That's right. And until they do materialise properly, I can't trace the wave back to its source and Time Loop it.'

'But you've got access to the greatest source of knowledge in the universe.'

'Well, I know I talk to myself, sometimes . . .'

Andred pointed to the Circlet perched on the head of the blissfully absorbed K9. 'I was referring to the Matrix.'

'Oh, that old thing,' said the Doctor disparagingly. He staggered and clutched at the TARDIS console for support. Suddenly, Andred realised that the Doctor was on the point of complete exhaustion, sustained only by sheer will-power.

'Sorry,' said the Doctor apologetically. 'Been under a bit of strain recently. Well, that's the problem, you

86

see, the Matrix has been invaded too. It's not safe for me to use it.'

'Why didn't you just explain to the Supreme Council——'

'*Because the Vardans can read my thoughts*. That's why I've plugged K9 into the Matrix, he's got no brain, not in the organic sense ... sorry about that, K9, no offence.'

'Can you trust a machine with so much knowledge?'

'This one I can, he's my second-best friend. Aren't you K9?' K9 was too busy to answer.


Kelner was telling the Vardans of the death of the rebel guards, and of the hunt for Andred. 'There is one other matter, sir,' he concluded. 'Unfortunately, it is a matter of the utmost delicacy.'

'Speak.'

'The President has been acting just a little oddly. For instance, at the moment he seems to have locked himself into an old time capsule. It is a little strange, don't you think, sir?'

'We wondered how long it would take you to recognise and report this. You have just passed the first test of your loyalty to us.'

'You knew that the Doctor was not reliable?'

'We shall be ready to deal with the Doctor very soon. We have suspected him ever since he first made contact with us. It was too convenient ...'


'Well, at least they don't suspect me yet,' said the Doctor hopefully. 'Banishing Leela and the others made quite a good impression, I think. Anyway, it was the only way I could protect them. Give me your helmet, Andred.'

87

'What?'

'Your helmet man.'

Andred took the helmet from his head and handed it over.

The Doctor peered inside. 'Well, it might work. Not much room, though.' Clutching the helmet he disappeared through the inner door without another word.

Andred rubbed his eyes. 'Well, one of us must be mad! And if it isn't him . . .'

Still busily absorbing data, K9 made no comment.

The squad leader concluded his report. 'We've managed to arrest most of the Chancellor's Guard, sir. But there's still no sign of Commander Andred himself. We think he may have escaped to the Outside.'

'That is most unsatisfactory,' said the Vardan softly.

Kelner smiled. 'Don't worry, sir, he won't survive long out there. No one does!'

An arrow thudded into a distant target, and there was scattered applause from the mixed group of Outsiders and Time Lords gathered outside the hut. 'Well shot, Leela,' said Nesbin.

Leela shrugged. 'It is a good weapon—but we shall need many more.'

'We will if we're going to feed all this lot.' By now Nesbin was almost embarrassed by the number of his followers. Expelled Time Lords were joining the Outsiders daily. Rodan was in charge of a kind of reception committee set up to find them as soon as they were expelled and bring them to safety.

'The weapons will be needed for war, not for hunting,' said Leela.

'We can't fight an alien invasion with bows and arrows!'

'Why not?' Leela sent another arrow thudding into the target.

She beckoned one of the younger Time Lords. 'Here, you try.' The Time Lord came reluctantly forward and took the bow. He drew and fired, nearly ending the life of old Gomer who stood watching some considerable distance from the target. Nesbin covered his eyes with his hands and groaned. He shoved the Time Lord aside, and beckoned another. 'Here, you try.'

They tried Time Lord after Time Lord with the bow. Only one hit the target, and he shot with his eyes closed. They tested the Time Lords with knives and spears and clubs, until finally Nesbin lost patience and chased them all off with roars of anger.

Leela shook her head despairingly. 'Not one of them is any use with any kind of weapon.'

Nesbin said gloomily. 'So much for your army.'

Leela wasn't dismayed for long. 'We shall just have to attack on our own?'

'Who will?'

'You, me, the best of your hunters. Sometimes a small, swift force is best.'

'There aren't enough of us to capture the Capitol. The Castellan's bodyguard will all be armed with stasers.'

'We shall not try to capture the Capitol, merely to rescue the Doctor. He will tell us what to do after that.'

Nesbin scratched his head. 'But according to these Time Lords, your Doctor's on the side of the invaders.'

'That is impossible,' said Leela flatly. 'We must rescue him. Choose your best warriors, Nesbin. Rodan will come with us to guide us within the Capitol.'

89

Grumbling, Nesbin started to select his men.


The Doctor dashed back into the TARDIS control room and clapped the helmet on Andred's head. 'There, that should keep them guessing.'

The helmet felt strange and it didn't seem to fit. Andred took it off and peered inside. Built into the crown was a small but complex piece of electronic circuitry.

'I've built in a partial encephalographic barrier,' explained the Doctor. 'It'll keep most of your thoughts a secret, but you'll have to concentrate.'

K9 raised his head. 'Master, I have located the wave-channel being used by the invaders. It is an outer spatial exploration and investigation channel, number 87656432 positive. Unfortunately, I cannot detect where it is tuned to as there is considerable interference. Probability of deliberate jamming, nine five per cent.'

The Doctor sighed. 'So, I've still got to persuade them to materialise, before we can trace their origin, which means they'll have to trust me, which means I'll *have* to dismantle the force-field around Gallifrey. It's the only way I can convince them I'm really on their side.'

Andred was horrified. 'But you can't dismantle the force-field, not without blowing the planet to pieces.'

'I can't, but perhaps Rassilon can.'

'Rassilon?'

'Why not? He's the greatest Time Lord scientist there's ever been, and he set up the force-field in the first place.'

Andred decided it must be the Doctor who was mad. 'Rassilon is *dead*, he's been dead for millions of years.'

'Maybe so—but his mind lives on, remember, as part of the Matrix.'

'Dismantle the force-field and the whole of Gallifrey will be helpless,' protested Andred.

'Exactly,' said the Doctor cheerfully. 'That's why it's such a good way to convince the Vardans don't you think?' Before Andred could reply the Doctor said, 'That's the spirit! K9 you're in charge.'

'But——' said Andred.

The Doctor was gone.

'I am in charge,' said K9 importantly. 'We will retrace the invasion circuit and fuse it.'

'That circuit is used by the Academy for instruction in exploration.'

Astonishingly for an automaton K9 made a joke. 'Then we will give them a day off school!'


As the Doctor entered the great hall of the Panopticon, he was not surprised to see that the shimmering forms of three Vardans awaited him on the central platform.

He climbed the ramp to meet them, the Circlet in his hand. 'I've been thinking about our little problem,' he began.

'And you need to consult the Matrix? We know, Doctor.'

The Doctor was scarcely surprised. He had been careful to keep the idea in his mind ever since leaving the TARDIS, and as he had expected, the Vardans had monitored his mind, and arrived before him.

'Well, if you'll excuse me ...' The Doctor put the Circlet on his head. His body went rigid, and he stood motionless for what seemed a long time. At last, with an effort, he raised the Circlet from his head, the signs of strain clearly marked upon his face.

'There is a way, but it is difficult and dangerous.'

91

The Vardan said, 'Proceed, Doctor. But remember, we can read your every thought!'

Deep beneath the Capitol was a secret, long-disused control room. When the Doctor arrived there, he found one of the Vardans awaiting him.

The room was packed with complex, incredibly ancient equipment, long-disused. No one had dared tamper with the quantum force field, since it had been set up in the days of the great Rassilon himself.

The Doctor studied the controls, row upon row, bank upon bank of them. 'Difficult, very difficult,' he said. 'But not impossible!' He set to work, touching a control here, adjusting another there, dismantling several consoles re-connecting them in what seemed a very haphazard manner. He worked slowly at first, then with increasing confidence. He turned to the watching Vardan. 'Don't stare like that, you're making me nervous. This is a very delicate operation, you know!' At last the Doctor stood back, rubbing his eyes wearily. 'Now, this is the tricky bit. I've re-connected the circuitry, and I'm about to feed in full power. Hold your breath, or whatever Vardans do!'

Slowly he pulled back the master power-switch.

The control room, the entire Capitol, and a large part of Gallifrey itself began to shudder and vibrate. The effect was strange and horrifying. Solid matter, walls, ceilings, floors, seemed to ripple like water, to shift and wave like the ever-moving sea.

Distant cries of alarm could be heard from all over the Capitol.

Kelner in his office, Leela and her band of warriors creeping stealthily towards the Capitol, even Andred hiding in the TARDIS felt the strange wave-like effect.

In the control room the Doctor worked frantically at the improvised set-up trying to check and control the incredibly powerful planetary forces he had unleashed. 'Hang on,' he shouted. 'Nearly there ...'

The rumbling died away, matter became solid again, everything was normal.

(In the TARDIS K9 looked up. 'The Doctor has succeeded. Imperative we reach president's office immediately. Come!')

When the Doctor strode back into the Panopticon, a trembling Kelner was awaiting him, three Vardan projections grouped around him. 'There you are,' said the Doctor breezily. 'Well, I did it!'

Even the Vardan Leader seemed impressed.

'You have dismantled the quantum force-field?'

'It's impossible to dismantle the force-field without vaporising the planet. What I have done is made a sizeable hole in it, directly above the Capitol.'

'You have done well,' said the Vardan slowly. 'Now all our forces can be projected from our planet. Gallifrey is ours.'

Kelner gave the Doctor a frightened look. 'A hole in the force-field? Then we're unprotected!'

'You have our protection now,' said the Vardan ironically. 'Are you not satisfied, Castellan?'

'Yes, yes, of course,' said Kelner hurriedly. 'This hole, Doctor—is it permanent?'

'Not yet. I'll have to make a few more adjustments to get the balance completely stable, or the force-field will re-establish itself.'

The Vardans stood silent, as if receiving some distant signal. Far above, the Vardan flag-ship was slowly descending towards the Capitol.

As the ship passed the force-field level unharmed the Vardan Leader turned and said exultantly. 'It is done. We are safe now.' The Vardans began to materialise.

93

# 10

## False Victory

Kelner stared in astonishment, as the three shimmering shapes were replaced by three solid forms.

He stared at the Vardans in a kind of astonished disappointment.

The Vardans were human—or humanoid at least.

Three tall, stern faced men in drab green battledress, belts cluttered with pouches and equipment, helmets on their heads.

They carried no weapons, but they did not need them. The Vardan flag-ship hovered above the Capitol. The merest thought-impulse could see the Vardans whisked back to safety and the Capitol blasted to dust.

Kelner said dully, 'But they're just ordinary humanoids ...'

'That's right,' said the Doctor. 'Disappointing, isn't it?' He nodded affably to the Vardans. 'Nice to see you again.'

'You have work to do, Doctor,' said the Vardan Leader coldly. 'Continue with it. One of us will assist you.'

'Oh, I can manage nicely, thanks all the same.'

'Accompany him!' ordered the Leader and one of his two companions moved to the Doctor's side.

'Tell you what,' suggested the Doctor brightly. 'Why don't you assist me in my work?'

A Vardan close behind him, the Doctor left the Panopticon.

*

94

Leela halted her band on the edge of the Capitol. Its sheer white walls looming above them. 'Nesbin, you and your men move on to the far side. Attack the guards, make them think it is a mass attack. I shall slip through the other way with Jasko and Rodan.'

Nesbin nodded, and led the bulk of the force away.

Leela, Rodan, and a burly young Outsider called Jasko set off for the nearby tunnel to the Capitol. Jasko wasn't especially bright, but he was brave and strong, and he knew how to obey orders.

Rodan knew the control codes that opened the tunnel door—clearly no one had bothered to change them. They came through the tunnel, out into the corridor. They didn't see a living soul. No Time Lords, no guards, no Vardans, no one.

'Something's wrong,' whispered Leela. 'It's all too easy. We must move carefully.'

They crept on their way.


The Doctor led his Vardan guard not to the control room, but back to the president's office.

'Why do we come here?' asked the Vardan suspiciously.

The Doctor smiled disarmingly. 'Shan't keep you a moment old chap, I've forgotten my hat.'

Before the Vardan had time to realise that the Doctor was wearing his hat, he had opened the door, slipped inside, and slammed it. The Vardan reached for the door handle to follow and heard the sound of heavy bolts being slammed home. He tried to open the door, found he could not move it, and promptly dematerialised intending to materialise on the other side. To his astonishment, he found it was impossible —he simply re-appeared in the corridor. Angrily, the Vardan disappeared again.

Inside the office, the Doctor guessed what had happened and grinned. 'No use trying that one, old chap.' He patted the door with its ornately carved lead screen, and turned to find Andred and K9 staring at him. 'So pleased you could both make it.' The Doctor waved around the lead-lined room. 'Nothing like lead, is there. Good old base lead.'

'Insulation,' said Andred realising. 'This room is insulated against the Vardans.'

'That's right. Come on K9, we've got a lot to do!'

The baffled Vardan re-materialised inside the Panopticon and reported to his leader, who rounded upon Kelner. 'The Doctor has betrayed us. Kill him. You are now in charge here. I must have discipline!'

Kelner felt his moment had come. 'I shall take control immediately.'

Despite Leela's fears, she and her two friends had reached the TARDIS unopposed. Now Jasko and Rodan stood watching as Leela hammered on the door.

'Suppose he isn't in there?' asked Jasko.

Leela turned impatiently to Rodan. 'If he's not in here, where else would he be?'

'Well, he is the President isn't he? I suppose he could be in the President's office.'

'Take us there!'

The little party set off again.

From the safety of his office, Kelner was despatching his men to capture the Doctor, an event he had no intention of attending in person. 'This order is to be

96

expedited immediately. I assume complete authority. The President will be shot on sight!'

The Doctor took the Rod of Rassilon from his pocket and handed it casually to Andred. 'Hold this a minute will you?'

Reverently, Andred took the sacred Rod.

'And this!' The Doctor took the Circlet from the other pocket and passed it over. He unfastened the Sash of Rassilon. 'This too!'

Astonished and overawed, Andred stood holding Gallifrey's equivalent of the Crown Jewels, while the Doctor grabbed K9 round the middle and with a grunt of effort set him upon the Presidential desk.

He took the Rod, the Sash and the Circlet from Andred, looped the Sash and the Circlet over K9's head, and thrust the Rod between them.

Andred tried to protest, but the Doctor said soothingly. 'Just trust me. Ready, K9?'

'Affirmative!'

'Then do as you've been told.'

There was a tremendous thud from outside, then another and another. Someone, several someones by the sound of it, was raining heavy blows on the other side of the door.

A picked squad of Kelner's bodyguard had been issued with the heavy ceremonial axes carried in Gallifreyan ceremonial parades. Now they were busily trying to smash down the door of the Presidential office with clumsy old-fashioned weapons that had never been intended for serious use. Despite the fact that a watching Vardan was urging them on, it was taking them quite a time. Work became even slower when two of

97

the axe-squad suddenly dropped, transfixed by arrows. Leela had arrived.

Leela and Jasko fired again, two more men fell, the Vardan dematerialised and the attack was over.

Leela glared at the space left by the vanishing Vardan. 'What was that?'

'Someone vanishing,' said Rodan unhelpfully.

'Is this the President's office?'

Rodan nodded.

Leela snatched up an axe. 'Then let us break the door down!' She began hammering at the door. 'Doctor,' she yelled. 'Do not fear, we come to save you!'

The Doctor groaned at the sound of the familiar voice. 'I might have guessed. Let her in, Andred!'

Andred drew the bolts.

Waving axes, Leela and her two friends tumbled into the room. 'Doctor!' said Leela delightedly.

'Shut up, Leela,' said the Doctor. 'Ready, K9? Now!'

K9 began to whirr and click and buzz in the most alarming fashion, as he called on the mighty forces now at his disposal. His eyes glowed, his antennae quivered. Leela, Andred and the others watched in silent astonishment.


Inside the Panopticon, the Vardan War Leader stiffened in sudden alarm. 'Alert! Alert! I detect an unauthorised frequency tracer. Alert! Full Alert!'


'Contact!' said K9 suddenly. 'Co-ordinates of Vardan home planet are Vector three zero five two alpha seven, fourteenth span.'

The Doctor's voice was suddenly urgent. 'Activate Modulation Rejection Pattern, Time Loop mode.'

98

'Activating—now!'

Kelner ran into the Panopticon, eager to report that the Doctor was trapped in the Presidential office, his capture only a matter of time, and then paused in astonishment. The three Vardans stood in a tight group in the centre of the dais. As he watched they blurred, shimmered—and disappeared!

High above the Capitol, the Vardan space ship vanished too.

In the President's office there was complete and utter silence. Everyone was watching K9.

At last he spoke. 'Wave pattern negative, repeat, negative. No trace of Vardan life-form on Gallifrey.'

Slowly, very slowly, the Doctor got up. He began removing the regalia from K9, taking off Rod, Sash and Circlet, and handing them to Andred.

'What happened?' asked Leela.

'We've won,' said the Doctor gently.

'Won?'

'Yes. I've sent the Vardans back home—to stay.'

Leela sounded almost disappointed. 'But we have fought only a few guards and some cowardly thing that vanished. How have we won?'

'It's not always like Waterloo, or the relief of Mafeking, you know,' said the Doctor wearily. 'This was a battle of intellect, of technology.'

'All right, all right,' said Leela. 'I'll take your word for it.'

They went out into the corridor, and the Doctor looked down at the four arrow-pierced guards. 'Have

99

you ever thought of taking up killing people seriously, Leela? If you set your mind to it, you could become quite proficient! Come on, let's see what's going on!'

He headed for the Panopticon.

'Proficient,' muttered Leela. 'What does proficient mean?' She wasn't sure if she was being complimented or insulted.

The Doctor entered the great hall of the Panopticon, to find no one there except Kelner, who bowed before him, wringing his hands. 'Doctor! President! Sir!' he cried in anguish.

'Confusing, isn't it?' said the Doctor amiably. 'Is the Chancellor still in his office?'

Kelner had almost forgotten old Borusa, put under house arrest such a very long time ago. 'As far as I know, sir.'

'I shall want to see him, immediately.'

'Yes, Excellency.'

'Kelner, as Castellan you are responsible for the security of Gallifrey in general, and for my safety in particular, aren't you?'

'Yes, Excellency.'

The Doctor shook his head. 'I don't think you're very good at it,' he said sadly. 'Mind you, that's only my opinion. Every oligarchy gets the Castellan it deserves, eh, Castellan?'

Kelner was too frightened to reply. Clearly, he expected immediate execution at the very least. The Doctor sighed. 'Never mind. Just clear up the mess when you've a moment or two.'

Kelner retreated bowing.

Andred hurried into the room, and saluted the Doctor. 'Victory, Your Excellency,' he called exultantly.

100

The Doctor gave a weary but triumphant smile. 'Victory it is,' he said solemnly. 'It has been a long hard fight, but the safety of Gallifrey has been assured.'

He became aware of a sudden silence. Instead of giving three rousing cheers, they were all staring fixedly over his shoulder.

The Doctor turned.

Three strange figures stood in the doorway, watching him. Not the vanquished Vardans, but three very different figures.

They wore shining space armour. They were short and squat with immensely wide shoulders, broad powerful limbs, and great dome-shaped helmets.

The leader of the three figures removed his helmet to reveal a face from some ancient nightmare. The head was huge and round and it seemed to emerge directly from the massive shoulders. The hairless skull was greeny-brown and small red eyes were set deep in cavernous sockets. The nose was a snubby snout, the wide mouth a lipless slit.

It was the face of a Sontaran.

# 11

## The Sontarans

The Sontaran held a slubby hand-blaster aimed unerringly at the Doctor.

'Please don't fire that thing,' said the Doctor mildly.

'Pointless killing is unproductive. Slavery is more functional.' The Sontaran's voice was a harsh, guttural whisper.

'What are these things?' whispered Leela.

'Sontarans.'

'You know them?'

'Oh yes, I know them.' The Doctor had encountered Sontarans before. They were a savagely militaristic species with only one interest—war! In the intervals of their unending war with their deadly enemies the Rutans, the Sontarans occasionally turned their attention to other species. The Doctor had foiled their plans before, once in Earth's medieval past, and once in its far distant future.

I should have known, thought the Doctor wearily. The Vardans were only the forerunners, the puppets. They had the technological skills, but not the savagely militaristic will for an operation such as this. Only the Sontarans would dare to attempt the greatest military coup in the galaxy. The conquest of Gallifrey—the invasion of Time itself!

The Sontaran announced, 'I am Commander Stor of the Sontaran Special Space Service.'

'Isn't that carrying alliteration a little too far?'

Commander Stor ignored the Doctor's joke. Son-

102

tarans have no sense of humour, though they occasionally smile at the death-throes of an enemy.

'What about the Vardans?' asked Leela. 'They were your allies?'

'The Vardans were expendable. They served their purpose—to open the force-field and let *us* in.'

Typical Sontaran ruthlessness, thought the Doctor almost admiringly. How like the Sontarans to use an entire species for their shock troops—and sacrifice them without a second thought in the cause of Sontaran victory.

Commander Stor said suddenly, 'Which one is "Dok-tor"? Are you "Dok-tor"?' The name sounded strange in the harsh alien voice.

The Sontaran looked at Kelner who said hurriedly, 'Oh, no!' and shot a quick betraying glance at the Doctor.

The Sontaran swung round. 'You, then?'

'I am Lord President of the Supreme High Council of the Time Lords of Gallifrey,' announced the Doctor loftily.

'Your description matches one called "Dok-tor", an enemy of the Sontaran race.'

'I can't help that, can I? I'm the Lord President of Gallifrey. You may address me as "sir".'

Stor raised his blaster and fired. The Doctor writhed in agony, as a red haze enveloped his body. 'I call no one "sir" but my military superiors,' said the Sontaran dispassionately.

The red haze disappeared, leaving the Doctor weak and shaken. 'That must mean several thousand sirs,' he muttered.

'Thousand? The glorious Sontaran army reckons its numbers in hundreds of millions.' Stor turned to one of his aides. 'Find the one called, "Dok-tor" and kill him.'

The Sontaran raised an arm in salute and marched away.

Cardinal Borusa sat at his desk in the Chancellor's office, a tiny intercom unit in his hand. The Doctor's voice came from the speaker. 'I was only trying to help.'

Borusa switched off the intercom and sat lost in thought. He had been confined to his suite of offices in the Chancellery ever since his confrontation with the Vardans, regaining his strength and awaiting an opportunity to help the Doctor. He had been woken from an uneasy sleep by the noise and confusion in the Capitol, and soon realised that his guard had disappeared. In an attempt to find out what was going on, Borusa had monitored the conversation in the Panopticon. He had just been about to emerge and congratulate the Doctor on his victory when the arrival of this new threat made him decide to stay in hiding. Borusa switched on the com-unit.

The Doctor was still managing to hold the Sontaran in talk. 'I take it you have invaded Gallifrey in search of knowledge, Commander Stor? Knowledge must always be the ultimate goal, must it not?'

'A means to an end only. The ultimate goal is victory.'

'Victory over whom?'

'Victory over all!'

'Victory over time?' suggested the Doctor.

There was sudden suspicion in the harsh alien voice. 'What did you say?'

'Do you seek victory over time itself?'

Borusa knew that the words held a message for him. The Doctor had realised that he would be listening,

104

and was warning him of the Sontaran plans. Borusa smiled, and his hand went to a control panel set into the desk top.

In the Panopticon, Stor had sensed that he was being delayed, and had become uneasy. 'Enough of this idle talk. When my troops arrive you will all be placed in confinement——'

An indescribable noise filled the Panopticon. It was a high-pitched, howling, screaming, reverberating chime. It assaulted the ear with intolerable force.

The Doctor clapped his hands over his ears and yelled, 'Run!'

No one could hear what he was saying, but the Doctor's friends instinctively followed him as he sprinted from the hall.

Sontaran hearing is surprisingly sensitive, and Stor seemed to be affected worse than anyone else. Gauntleted hands clutching his head he reeled in agony.

Kelner, anxious to ingratiate himself with this new regime went to help him. He got in the way of a flailing arm and was sent spinning across the hall.


The Doctor pounded along the corridor with Leela, Rodan, Andred, two of Andred's men and an Outsider called Jablif close behind him. Suddenly the howling noise stopped and the Doctor realised it was time to stop running and start making plans. He raised a hand. 'Stop!'

Everyone stopped. They all began shaking their heads and rubbing their ears.

'What was that noise?' gasped Leela.

'Celebration chimes. Should have been played at my election about fifty times quieter! I think someone's trying to help me.'

'We all are,' said Leela. 'What do we do next?'

'Follow me.'

'Where to?'

'My office. I've got an urgent appointment!'

Kelner scrambled to his feet, and immediately began to grovel. 'I am sorry, Lord Stor, this was none of my doing...'

Stor was rasping orders into his communicator. 'To all advance units. The President is to be apprehended. You may kill those with him, but take the President alive!'

Kelner said timidly, 'But surely you realise, the President is——'

'Silence!' roared Stor, and Kelner obeyed.

The Doctor stopped at a corridor junction flattening himself against the wall. 'Look out—a Sontaran!'

They heard the clumping of heavy booted feet, and a squat, menacing figure appeared at the other end of the corridor.

Leela drew her knife. 'Do not worry, Doctor, I will kill him.'

'You don't know how!'

'Then tell me.'

'There's a small opening at the back of their necks called the probic vent. It's their only weak point.'

'That is all I need to know.'

Leela cupped her hands to her mouth and gave a weirdly high-pitched call. 'Over hee ... eee ... re ...'

The sound echoed through the corridors, in such a way that it was impossible to tell where it was coming from. The Sontaran wheeled ponderously round, searching. Leela drew back her knife. The moment the Sontaran's back was fully turned, she threw.

The knife streaked through the air and buried itself deep in the probic vent. The Sontaran fell, dying without a sound.

'Leela,' said the Doctor solemnly, 'that was a prodigious throw!'

'Prodigious?'

The Doctor smiled. 'Amazing! And so was the way you tricked him, that cry ...'

'It was nothing, just——'

The Doctor grinned. 'I know, just an old hunting trick. Come on.'

Pausing only to wrench her knife from the Sontaran's neck, Leela followed him.


Since most of Stor's command had yet to arrive, he had relatively few troopers at his command, and those few were dispersed about an incredibly large complex of buildings. He was doing his best to direct them by remote control. 'Unit three seven, report.' There was no reply. Stor swung menacingly round on Kelner. 'One of my troopers has failed to report. Therefore he is dead.'

A hand like a clamp grabbed Kelner's arm. 'Where will they be heading?'

'Level three is on the way to level five,' whimpered Kelner. 'They must be making for the president's office.'

Stor spoke into the communicator. 'Units three, five and seven proceed immediately to level five. Intercept the President and his bodyguard. Take him alive.'

'My lord, I don't think you realise——' began Kelner.

'Silence! Do not interfere, Time Lord!'

Kelner fell silent. He had been about to discuss that

the President was the Doctor, but he had no intention of arguing with an angry Sontaran.

'Come with me,' ordered Stor.

Meekly Kelner followed him.

The Doctor shot along the corridor and opened the door to his office. Already he could hear the pounding feet of Sontaran troopers. 'Come on now, this is the dangerous bit.'

Leela, Andred, Rodan and the two guards hurried through the door and the Doctor counted them in. 'Five, four, three, two, one ... One, two, three, four, five, no more.' He slammed the door behind him and bolted it.

He turned to find his friends huddled together in a group. Cardinal Borusa was covering them, and the Doctor, with a staser-pistol.

'I thought you would never get here,' said the old man in a conversational tone.

'We were delayed,' said the Doctor, equally calmly.

'Nothing too troublesome, I hope?'

The staser was steady in the old man's hand.

Commander Stor, Castellan Kelner, and a squad of Sontaran troopers converged outside the door to the Presidential office. Stor looked at Kelner. 'Is this the place, Time Lord?'

'Yes, Excellency.'

Stor gestured to his troopers, and they raised their blasters.

The Doctor looked thoughtfully at the lead-lined door. 'That's not going to keep them out for long is it Chancellor.'

'Easily fusible, malleable base metal such as lead is not the best defence against heat intensive weaponry,' said Borusa judicially. 'Fortunately, someone had the sense to re-inforce it with a titanium-based alloy.'

'Your recipe, Chancellor?'

'I had a feeling this office might someday need defending,' said Borusa. 'And it is not one of my duties to protect the president?'

'Dereliction of duty is sadly common these days,' said the Doctor. 'Or hadn't you noticed?' He looked pointedly at Borusa's staser.

'I was about to emerge to offer you my congratulations, Doctor. However, this new development——'

'Is even more of a surprise to me than it is to you.'

'And to your companions?'

'I vouch for them.'

'Of your own free will?'

'Yes.'

Borusa considered a moment longer. He handed the staser to the Doctor. 'I am at your command, Excellency.'

Leela scowled at the formidable old man, still not sure if he was friend or enemy. 'Shall I kill him now, Doctor?'

'No! I need all the friends I can get.'

'But he threatened you!'

The Doctor smiled. 'Nevertheless, you are a friend, aren't you Chancellor. The most important friend of all.'

Borusa bowed his head, aware of the hidden significance in the Doctor's words.


Stor glared disgustedly at the door. 'Not even scratched! Bring better weapons. Make sure they are effective, or I will negate you all!'

The terrified Sontaran troopers hurried away.

The Doctor sat on his desk and swung his legs. 'I imagine they'll be bringing up the heavy artillery pretty soon.'

'It would seem to be the next logical step,' agreed Borusa.

'And our most logical step would appear to be evacuation. I believe the exit through your office would be best, Chancellor. There's something in there I need rather badly.'

Borusa led the way to the door, and repeated the pass-word. The door swung open and they all filed through.

The Doctor tip-toed across the office and unbolted the main door. Picking up Borusa's staser he followed the others.

Stor heard a faint click and cocked his massive head. 'What is that?' Blaster in hand he moved cautiously forward and tried the door. It swung open. 'What trick is this?'

'I have no idea, sir,' quavered Kelner.

Stor shoved the door fully open and marched through. The room was empty.

In the Chancellor's office, the Doctor lifted K9 down from the desk. 'Leela, take K9 and the others back to the TARDIS. The Chancellor and I have vital matters to discuss.'

'Doctor, I will not leave you again,' said Leela fiercely. 'Every time I do, you get into trouble.'

'Quite right,' agreed the Doctor cheerfully, 'but just do as I ask.'

Leela knew there was no arguing with that tone. She led the others from the office.

'Activate, K9,' said the Doctor and the little automaton glided after them.

The Doctor handed the staser butt-first to Borusa. 'Well, Cardinal, it's time you made up your mind. Do you intend to help me—or kill me?'

## 12

## The Key of Rassilon

'I have no idea what you are talking about,' said Borusa calmly. 'I have already assured Your Excellency of my loyalty.'

'But you're still not *quite* sure, are you Chancellor? There's still some lingering vestige of doubt in the back of your mind, eh?'

'That is not so, Your Excellency.'

'Isn't it? *Then give me the Great Key of Rassilon!*' Borusa was silent.

'Well?' snapped the Doctor. 'Where is it?'

'You ask for the impossible.'

'I ask for the Great Key—the true Great Key,' said the Doctor implacably.

'You already have all the Circlet presidential regalia——'

'I have the Rod of Rassilon, and the Sash. I do not have the Key itself.'

'The Key was stolen by the Master, when he escaped from Gallifrey . . .'

'The Great Key of Rassilon, lying unguarded in a museum?' The Doctor shook his head. 'That was a facsimile, a lesser key. Good enough for the Master's purposes—but not the Grey Key itself.'

The old man was silent.

'Listen to me, Borusa,' said the Doctor fiercely. 'People are dying in this battle. Isn't that important to you?'

'Should it be?'

'It leaves you unmoved, doesn't it?' said the Doctor softly. 'That's the difference between us, Chancellor. I *am* concerned, very much concerned.'

'Then perhaps you should remember your training in detachment.'

'I do—but I prefer to care. Don't you care about the invasion of Gallifrey by Sontaran shock troops. Just a few of them now, but soon there will be millions, invading time itself.'

The Doctor's angry words produced an equally fierce response. 'They cannot invade time. Not while I——' Borusa bit off his words.

'Not while you have the Great Key,' completed the Doctor softly. 'Where is it, Chancellor?'

Borusa rose stiffly, and touched a control on his desk. A screen slid back to reveal a velvet display case, holding not one but at least a hundred keys. The keys were of all shapes and sizes, some huge and ornate, others hardly more than plain metal rods.

The Doctor smiled. 'If you wanted to hide a tree, where better than in a forest? I remember that from one of your lectures. Which one is it?'

Unable to face the surrender of this last secret, Borusa did not reply.

'I understand how you feel,' said the Doctor gently. 'Rassilon was a wily old bird, wasn't he? No president can have total power without the Great Key, isn't that so? To protect the Time Lords from dictatorship, he gave the Great Key into—other hands.'

'None of this information is in the Matrix,' protested Borusa.

'I know, I've been there, remember? There is no record in the Matrix of any president knowing the whereabouts of the Great Key. So who does know? Not the Castellan, he's only a jumped-up guard. And who guards the guards?'

113

Borusa bowed his head in assent. 'The Chancellor

'That's right,' said the Doctor quietly. 'It had t be you. It is my duty to kill you, if it will prevent tha Key falling into the hands of the Sontarans.'

Borusa gave him a wintry smile. 'That will not b necessary.' He took a key, by no means the largest o the most impressive, from the forest of keys in the cas and handed it to the Doctor. 'You are the first presiden since Rassilon himself to hold the Great Key.'


Leela and her friends were fighting their way toward the TARDIS. Just before they reached the ant chamber they had run straight into a Sontaran patro Both sides took cover, and stasers crackled and blaster roared as both sides opened fire.

Leela and her Gallifreyans fought gallantly, but th Sontarans were trained shock troops, they had heav duty blasters, and the stasers carried by Leela an her friends were ineffective against Sontaran spac armour.

Only K9 had the necessary fire power. Methodicall he blasted down one Sontaran after another.

Nevertheless, the Gallifreyans were being defeated Leela decided there was only one thing to do—attack Using K9 as a spearhead, she and Andred led a des perate charge in an attempt to break through the Son taran cordon and reach the safety of the TARDIS.

Andred and Rodan managed to follow K9 to safety but the loyal guards were shot down in the fighting and Jablif, the Outsider fell, badly wounded.

Leela had been holding back acting as a rearguard She hurried to Jablif's side, pulling him back into th shelter of an alcove. 'Leave me, Leela,' he growled 'Save yourself!'

Leela tried to drag him after the others. But Jabli

114

was a heavy man, and he was too badly wounded to help her.

'You can't help me now, Leela, and they need you,' he gasped. 'Now go!'

Reluctantly Leela left him, and ran after the others.

Jablif slumped back as if unconscious, but as the Sontaran troopers ran past him in pursuit of Leela he raised himself upon one elbow. His arm flashed back, and a Sontaran fell, Jablif's knife embedded deep in his probic vent.

The next Sontaran finished Jablif off with a burst of blaster fire and ran on leaving Jablif dead beside the Sontaran he had killed.

The surviving Sontarans thundered after Leela but they were too late. Andred, Rodan, K9 and Leela were already safe inside the TARDIS.


In the President's office Kelner had finally succeeded in impressing Stor with the fact that the missing president was also the 'Dok-tor!' he sought.

'Why did you not tell me this before, Time Lord,' growled Stor menacingly.

'I tried, but you wouldn't listen,' babbled Kelner. 'He called himself the Doctor for many life-spans, even before he became president ... I never trusted him, even when your friends the Vardans paid us their all-too-brief visit. It was the Doctor who got rid of them you know, trapped them in a time loop ...'

'The Vardans were fools,' said Stor dismissively. 'But they had their uses—for a time.' The massive hand clamped onto Kelner's arm. 'And so may you, Time Lord.'

They were interrupted by a bleep from Stor's communicator. He listened to the message in mounting rage, and when he turned on Kelner, his voice was throaty with anger. 'The gap in the force-field is reclosing. My ship is trapped—it cannot land on Gallifrey!' As the Doctor had prophesied, the quantum force-field was regenerating itself.

Stor advanced menacingly on Kelner. 'You will re-open the gap in your force-field.'

'But I can't Excellency.'

'Liquidate him,' ordered Stor and turned away. A Sontaran trooper advanced on Kelner, blaster raised.

'Please, no,' screamed Kelner. 'I'd help you if I could, but it's impossible. No one can connect with the Matrix without the Circlet, and the Doctor has that.'

'Bypass the Matrix! You must re-establish the gap in the force-field, widen it so that our battle fleet can come through.'

'But it's impossible ...'

'To the strong, everything is possible,' said Stor. 'I must have my reinforcements. I shall seek out "Dok-tor", he will lead me to the Great Key!'

'The Doctor has the Great Key? That's not possible!'

'What?' roared Stor.

'Well of course, everything's *possible*,' said Kelner hurriedly. 'And if you *can* find the Great Key—then I may be able to find a way to do what you ask ...'


The Doctor and Borusa strolled calmly towards the TARDIS, a couple of Time Lords out for a little stroll.

A Sontaran trooper tried to bar their path. 'Ah, there you are,' said the Doctor breezily. 'Got your new orders yet? Check with Commander Stor, he'll put you in the picture.'

By the time the trooper had got through to Stor, the

116

Doctor and Borusa had disappeared.

Appalled, the trooper heard Stor's angry voice over his communicator, 'Of course there are no new orders! Follow, and destroy them.'

The Sontaran ran after the Doctor and Borusa. By now they were at the far end of the long corridor. 'Stop!' he called.

The two Time Lords strolled on, paying absolutely no attention. The trooper raised his blaster and fired. Blaster bolts roared down the corridor—with absolutely no effect on the departing figures.

As they turned the corner, the Doctor said, 'The Great Key seems to have some unusual properties.'

'It has,' agreed Borusa, 'but not against elementary energy-particle assault.'

'Then why are we still alive?'

Borusa tapped a complex device attached to the belt of his robe. 'The chancellor's personal force-shield. Unfortunately it hasn't been used for generations, and the power-pack has run dangerously low. What do you think we should do now, Doctor?'

'Run!' said the Doctor simply, and they tore off down the corridor.

'This is really most undignified,' protested Borusa as they ran. 'I haven't run like this for centuries.'

'Out of condition, that's your problem,' puffed the Doctor. Wryly he noticed that old Borusa was running smoothly and easily, and didn't seem in the least out of breath.

They slowed their pace, and by the time they neared the anteroom, they were moving in cautious silence.

The Doctor peered cautiously into the anteroom. There was the TARDIS—and there was a patrol of Sontaran troopers, posted in ambush around the edge of the room.

The Doctor pointed. 'Can you make it across there?'

'I believe I am still capable of running a little further.'

'I don't mean you Chancellor, I mean the power-pack on that force-field.'

Borusa studied the readings. 'We might—with luck.'

The Doctor crossed his fingers. 'One, two, three—go!'

They sprinted across the anteroom towards the TARDIS. By the time the astonished Sontarans reacted they were there. Blaster fire crackled around the force-field as the Doctor fumbled for his key. 'Maybe I'm still too young for this sort of thing,' he panted.

'If you could hurry up and open the door,' suggested Borusa mildly.

'I can never find that wretched key when I need it—ah here we are!'

The Doctor opened the TARDIS door, and they disappeared thankfully inside.

Leela, Andred and Rodan rushed forward to greet them. There was a hurried exchange of news and greetings, which the Doctor soon cut short. 'Rodan, you're a technician, so you stand right there. Andred you go to room 1207. Straight out that door and it's the sixty-second on the right. You too, K9. I want you fully re-charged. Leela, take our guests to the VIP lounge, down the stairs, third level, sharp right and through the door marked, "No Entry". You can't miss it.' As Leela headed for the inner door the Doctor said, 'Oh, and Leela?'

'Yes, Doctor?'

'Look after this for me, will you?' He tossed her the Great Key.

Borusa was horrified. 'You can't give the Great Key into the keeping of an alien savage.'

'I just did.'

118

'You trust her so much?'

'Yes, I do. Be careful with that Leela, it's important.'

'I shall guard it with my life,' said Leela matter-of-factly, and disappeared.

The Doctor turned to Rodan. 'Now, what did you say your name was?'

'Rodan, Your Excellency.'

'How do you do?'

'As well as I can, Excellency.'

The Doctor grinned. 'Who could ask for more! What's your speciality?'

'Quasitronics.'

'Ah,' said the Doctor. 'I'm afraid I don't know much about that.'

'It's just a simple field study, Excellency,' began Rodan.

'I dare say it is a simple field study,' said the Doctor impatiently, 'but it's no use to us here. You wouldn't have a glimmer of astrophysics, would you?'

'Only a glimmer, Your Excellency.'

'Well, we're going to break all the rules, so you can forget all you ever learned. I want you to switch the primary and secondary stabiliser circuitry of my TARDIS into your secondary defence barrier.

Rodan was shocked. 'You actually want me to link your control to the main defence mechanism of Gallifrey?'

'That's right. Then we can close up the hole I made, and stop any Sontaran ships from coming through.'

Rodan sighed. 'I don't suppose you've got a sonic screwdriver?'

Kelner stared despairingly round the defence control room, still almost in ruins after K9's attack. 'So much damage,' he moaned, 'so much disorder...'

'I must have my re-inforcements!' growled Stor.

'There may be some way of patching control though,' said Kelner dubiously. 'But it will take time ...'

'My general insists on immediate entry,' said Stor throatily. 'If I cannot fulfill his orders, it will be my military duty to die. But before I die, *you* will die, Time Lord!'

Hastily Kelner set to work.


Rodan had disappeared underneath the TARDIS console, only her feet still visible.

'Are you all right down there?' called the Doctor.

Rodan's head popped up. 'Of course I am. Crimps please.'

'Crimps,' repeated the Doctor and fished a complex-looking tool from a jumbled electronic tool-box at his side. 'Are you sure you know what you're doing?'

'Of course I do. Five two lever!'

The Doctor found the lever and passed it down. He patted the TARDIS console consolingly. 'Now don't you worry old girl, this won't hurt a bit!'

As Rodan worked on, the Doctor said broodingly, 'Unless we can stop them, the Sontarans will rampage not only through this universe and this time, but all universes, and all times. Nasty thought, isn't it. So we've just got to stop them, you see, we've just got to.'

Rodan muttered something that sounded like 'inkle grooner'.

The Doctor passed her another tool. 'They're after the Sash of Rassilon, the Rod, and most especially the Great Key. Those three, linked into the Matrix, provide the sum total of Time Lord power. Yes, that's what they want all right!'

120

Rodan appeared from beneath the TARDIS console and said loudly, 'Junk!'

The Doctor stared at her.

'Junk,' repeated Rodan. 'This whole contraption is a load of junk!'

'You're talking about my TARDIS!'

Rodan grinned at him. 'It worked though, all the same!' She switched on the scanner. 'Look!'

A pattern of sinister shapes appeared on the screen. 'Arrow head, arrow wings, arrow shaft,' said the Doctor softly. 'A classic Sontaran formation. It's an entire battle fleet!'

'Whatever it is, it's outside the quantum force-field,' said Rodan triumphantly. 'The defence screens are working again! We're safe!'

The Doctor brooded over the screen. 'You haven't seen what a Sontaran battle fleet can do! Are you sure the defence screen will hold?'

Rodan nodded. 'Yes, Your Excellency. As long as the TARDIS is secure, you control the defence screens.'


Kelner straightened up from the tangled ruins of a control bank. 'It's useless. Primary, secondary and tertiary circuits are out of order.'

'Repair them,' said Stor remorselessly.

'It's not a question of repair, Excellency. The damaged circuits seem to have been by-passed. The only way of doing that is through a type forty capsule and the only one of those in operation at the moment is the one used by the President!'

' "Dok-tor" ' roared Stor. His fist smashed down on a control bank shattering it still further.

Fear sent Kelner's brain into over-drive. 'There may be an alternative. If I can by-pass his stabiliser circuits ...' With renewed energy, Kelner set to work.

Some time later he straightened up, eyes gleaming with sly malice. 'Let's try it, then. If it works, the Doctor is in for a very unpleasant surprise.' He began throwing a series of switches, one by one.

The patched up equipment began throbbing with power. Something was happening.

'Better, Time Lord, better!' whispered Stor.


The TARDIS control room began to blur and shimmer as though dematerialising from the inside.

'What's happening?' screamed Rodan.

'Someone's reversed our stabiliser banks!'

'That's impossible. Only a high-ranking Time Lord could do that.'

'It's that toad Kelner!'

'What's going to happen to us?'

'If this keeps up, we'll all be dematerialised. It's like being hurled straight into a Black Star!'

Rodan fell, unconscious. The Doctor clutched the console for support, as the TARDIS began to blur and spin. Reality was fading before his eyes ...

## 13

## Failsafe

The Doctor became aware that someone was shaking his shoulder. It was Leela. Somehow she had fought her way back to him through the shuddering, vibrating TARDIS.

'Leela, get Rodan out of here,' shouted the Doctor.

Leela began dragging Rodan towards the door.

The Doctor lurched over to the console and smashed his fist down on a transparent plastic cover. There was a fierce klaxon like hooting. Gradually the interior of the TARDIS returned to normal ...

Kelner studied instrument readings, and shook his head in disappointment. 'I'm afraid the Doctor was too quick for us.'

'What has happened,' demanded Stor.

'He's managed to re-stabilise—thrown the failsafe switch on his time capsule. It's fixed in its present state for eternity—or until he turns off the failsafe switch.'

'Then he is trapped!'

'Trapped, and the Great Key with him,' said Kelner sadly. 'I could have done so much with that Great Key.'

Stor interrupted Kelner's dreams of power. 'Can we enter his capsule?'

'I have entered probes for all Time Capsules,' said Kelner slowly. 'It ought to be possible.'

'Then fetch the relevant probes. We shall go to this TARDIS.'

The Doctor closed the door from the control room and locked it. He produced a small silver tube. 'Nobody can re-set the system without this in. Where are the others, Leela?'

'In the bathroom.'

'*The bathroom?* Leela, you mean to say you got lost? You, the great huntress, got lost!' Chuckling the Doctor led them away.

Supporting the still-dazed Rodan, Leela followed him. 'Well, it's bigger than it looks this TARDIS of yours,' she muttered sulkily.

The exterior door of the TARDIS sprang open, revealing Stor, a Sontaran trooper, and Castellan Kelner.

Stor stared contemptuously around him. 'This machine is obsolete.'

'It was withdrawn some time ago,' said Kelner defensively.

'Can you make the systems function again, so that we regain control of the defence systems?'

'I doubt it,' said Kelner gloomily.

'Later you will make it work, or you will die,' said Stor. 'But first we must capture "Dok-tor".'

The Sontaran trooper was trying to open the inner door without success. 'He has half-fastened it with some kind of locking device,' he reported.

'He is still trapped,' said Stor gloatingly. 'There may be many inner chambers, but this is the only way out, is that not so, Time Lord?' Kelner nodded miserably.

'I shall have the door open soon,' said the trooper.

'Then we have him,' said Stor exultantly. 'And he has the Great Key. I want Dok-tor captured unharmed, remember. I wish to deal with him personally.'


The Doctor was leading the way through semi-darkness down a seemingly endless stairway.

'Don't worry,' he said confidently, 'I've got a perfect sense of direction. We're close to store-room twenty-three-A if I'm not mistaken. Come on!'

Leela was almost certain that the Doctor *was* mistaken. 'Where are we going, Doctor?'

'To the workshop, where I sent Andred and K9.'

The Doctor led them through a gloomy maze of store-rooms and tunnels, chatting brightly all the while. 'You see the advantage of this antiquated TARDIS of mine is that it's fully equipped and completely reliable...'

'Completely?' said Leela meaningfully.

The Doctor coughed. 'Well, almost completely.'

They came to a metal tunnel and the Doctor said, 'Here we are, service tunnel three, sector two five. Nearly there!'

Some considerable time later they found themselves trailing wearily along a metal walkway and the Doctor said uneasily, 'It's odd, you know, but I could have sworn we'd been here before.'

'We have,' said Leela grimly. 'We're going round in circles, Doctor.'

'Nonsense, that must have been sector twenty-three-B. It's very like this one.'

They followed him down a flight of stairs. Rodan saying the whole place needed re-decoration, the Doctor protesting that he had more important things to deal with. They were still wrangling when they climbed some steps and reached the tunnel again.

'Doctor we have been here before,' insisted Leela.

'It's just an illusion. It's called déjà vu, very common with time travellers.'

'Tell him, Rodan,' said Leela wearily.

'She's right, Doctor. We've been this way before.'

'Nonsense! I know the way round the TARDIS like the back of my hand.' The Doctor gave the back of his hand a thoughtful look, and they set off again.

This time they emerged into an enormous conservatory, crowded with lush green vegetation and bright with tropical plants. The air was warm and humid, and they seemed to be under an enormous glass dome beneath a blazing sun. Leela was astonished, and even Rodan was taken aback.

The Doctor took it all for granted. He stared at an ornamental clock standing against one wall. 'Slow again,' he said reprovingly, and adjusted the hands. Then with a sigh of relief, he sank into a chair.

A Sontaran trooper hurried back into the control room carrying a long plastic tube filled with complex circuitry. Watched by the impatient Stor, he applied the end of the rod to the locked door. After a moment the rod began to glow as a colossal flow of energy was channelled through it.

Kelner, meanwhile, had completed his examination of the TARDIS console. 'I'm sorry, sir, but it's impossible to reactivate. The Doctor has removed a primary refraction tube from the failsafe control. With that circuit missing, no one can do anything to the TARDIS.'

'So,' hissed Stor. 'I cannot destroy the TARDIS and the Doctor cannot escape. Stalemate! Trooper, how much longer to open that door?'

'Not long, sir, I'm very nearly through ...'


The Doctor jumped to his feet. 'Come on, we can't lounge about here all day.'

Leela sighed. 'Doctor, you just said you wanted a rest.'

'I've just had one! Let's go and see K9, he should be re-charged by now.'

It took a little more wandering and wrangling, but at last they found their way into the workshop, an enormous room filled with benches, lathes, and equipment for making or repairing practically anything. K9 was standing by close to a power socket, antenna plugged in patiently absorbing energy.

'Andred was standing over him. 'If I had a dog like you in my unit, K9, I'd make him a sergeant!'

'Hello, boy,' said the Doctor cheerfully. 'How's it going?'

'Nothing is going anywhere Master,' pointed out K9 with an automaton's logic. 'We are in a state of perfect inertia!'

'I don't really like the idea of inertia being perfect...'

Leela knelt beside K9 and patted his head.

'Is he ready?' asked the Doctor.

Andred nodded. 'Re-charged to capacity, just as you ordered, Doctor.'

'Good.'

A light flashed on the wall, and a buzzer sounded.

'What's that?' asked Leela.

'Early warning system. They've broken through the door downstairs.'


Squat and menacing, Stor stood for a moment in the

open doorway. He raised his helmet and set it upon his head. 'Now, Dok-tor, we shall do battle on your own ground.' Followed by his aide, Stor marched determinedly into the interior of the TARDIS.

K9 and the Doctor were deep in low voiced conversation. 'You understand, K9, you may pass on the information you have absorbed to Rodan, when I have prepared her—but to no one else.'

'Not even you, Master?'

'It's my plan K9, naturally I have to know about it! Leela, have you got the Key?'

Leela produced the Key and handed it to him.

'Look at me, Rodan!' commanded the Doctor softly. He stroked Rodan's forehead with his fingers, and she fell into a light hypnotic trance. 'Are you listening to me, Rodan.'

'Yes.'

'You will help, K9. You will carry out his instructions. When he asks you will give him his Key. You will give it to K9 or me, but to no one else, do you understand.'

'I understand.'

'Good! Watch the door will you Andred?'

The Doctor produced the Circlet and perched it on K9's head. 'It's up to you now, K9!'

'Master!'

'Leela, Andred, you come with me.'

'Where to?'

'To the bathroom, of course!'

The Doctor set off briskly, and the others followed.

Rodan turned and looked expectantly at K9. She looked bright and alert, and not in the least hypnotised.

K9 swivelled to face the rack of storage shelves. 'One

128

rod of type three iridium alloy, one metre in length. Five copper conduction discs.'

As K9 called out his weird shopping list, Rodan found the items he demanded and arranged them on a workbench.


Stor was descending the steps, followed by Kelner and a Sontaran trooper.

At the foot of the steps, Stor produced a device from his belt-pouch, studied the readings then put the little machine away in disgust. 'Very clever, Dok-tor.'

'What's happened?' asked Kelner nervously.

'The Doctor has set up a form of biological barrage, so that my tracking device cannot trace the life-forms of his party. Without the tracer we may never find him. We must return to the control room and destroy the barrier.'

'The barrage is probably powered by an ancilliary generator,' said Kelner. 'If I can find it, we can shut off the barrage.'

'Do this, and you will be well rewarded. Lead me to this device.'


What Leela referred to as the bathroom was in fact the swimming pool she had been using earlier. It was here that they found Borusa, stretched out comfortably on a low couch, calm and relaxed as always. 'Doctor!'

'There you are, Chancellor,' said the Doctor equally calmly. 'I'm sorry to disturb you, but I think you'd better come with us to somewhere a bit safer. Don't want you to fall into the hands of the Sontarans, do we. Terrible chaps! It's all a question of breeding, you know.'

Borusa rose and allowed the Doctor to lead him away. 'Surely, it isn't just their breeding which concerns you, Doctor?'

'Oh, but it is, I assure you. They breed at the rate of about a million a minute! This way Chancellor.' As they turned to leave, Stor and his trooper appeared at the far end of the room.

Stor raised his blaster and fired.

# 14

# The Chase

A second before the Doctor turned for a final glance round and saw the menacing figures just in time. 'Get down!' he yelled. Everyone ducked, and Stor's blaster-bolt crackled over their heads.

Before Stor could fire again, the Doctor and his group were through the end doors and haring down the corridor beyond.

Stor and the Sontaran trooper ran after them.

The Doctor led his party down a long corridor lined with doors. Suddenly the Doctor stopped. 'Wait! We'd better split up. Pick a door, any door!'

The Doctor, Borusa, Leela and Andred all ran through different doors and found themselves mysteriously all in the same place, a kind of mini-hospital with rows of curtained beds.

'I do wish you would stabilise your pedestrian infrastructure, Doctor,' said Borusa peevishly. 'Where are we now?'

'Sick bay?' The Doctor pointed to a door at the far end. 'Come on, Chancellor, we can get out this way. Lock the door Andred.'

The Doctor hurried Borusa down the ward. Andred locked and barred the door, Leela waiting beside him.

Andred slid the last of the heavy bolts. 'That should do it,' he said.

Stor smashed straight through the door, firing as he came.

A random bolt caught Andred's arm and sent him

flying across the room. Leela dived for cover beneath a bed.

Luckily for both of them, Stor and his trooper were more interested in the retreating forms of the Doctor and Borusa, who could just be seen disappearing through the far door. 'After them,' roared Stor.

Brushing aside the shattered fragments of the door frame, Stor thundered down the ward and out of sight, his trooper behind him.

Leela emerged from hiding and went over to Andred, who had rolled into a corner, clutching his wounded arm. She helped him to his feet. 'Come on, let's get out of here.'

'You go, Leela. I'll hold them off if they come back.'

'How?' asked Leela practically. 'Come on, we'll go this way.'

They went back through the door and into the corridor.

When they arrived in the conservatory, the Doctor and Borusa were waiting for them—rather to Leela's surprise, as she'd been certain the Doctor would get them lost again.

'Ah, there you are!' he called cheerfully. He noticed Andred clutching his arm, 'You're hurt, Andred. Is it bad?'

'Only a graze, Doctor but the arm's numb. I'm sorry, but I won't be much use for a while.' Andred's face was white with shock and it was clear it would take him some time to recover.

'Leela, you'd better take Andred and the Chancellor back to the workshop,' ordered the Doctor. 'Do you know the way this time?'

'I knew the way last time, Doctor.'

'Through that door there, sharp right, down two levels . . .'

132

Leela held up her hand. 'Please, no directions, Doctor. It will be easier without them!'

Leela led Andred and Borusa away, and the Doctor waited, considering his next move. The situation really didn't call for very much planning. All he had to do was stay alive until Rodan finished the task he had given her. But with Stor and his troopers rampaging round the TARDIS that might not be too easy.

Stor's blaster wouldn't work in the main control room of course, but the protective effect of the stabiliser field didn't extend to the rest of the ship. And even in the control room he wouldn't be safe, since Stor would be quite happy to throttle him or crush him to death.

Sontarans were appallingly strong, and the Doctor knew that if they once got their hands on him he would be done for.

The only thing to do he decided, was to carry on with this deadly game of hide and seek. The TARDIS was vast, and Stor had only a few troopers at his disposal. He should be able to keep them busy long enough for Rodan to finish her task.

Still considering the problem, the Doctor strolled around the conservatory. Except for a central path it was densely overgrown, a potted jungle, crammed with exotic plants from many different planets.

There were some very interesting species here, and some very dangerous ones too. The Doctor stopped before a huge, dense bush which carried not leaves but long trailing vine-like tentacles. As the Doctor approached, the vine-tentacles began to stir and wave, and seemed to reach out hungrily for him.

The Doctor smiled. 'You know, I think you might come in useful, old chap.'

He stopped, as he heard heavy footsteps. Someone

133

had come into the conservatory. Keeping well clear of the vine-plant, the Doctor ducked into the jungle.

The Sontaran trooper came cautiously down the path, domed head turning from side to side, blaster at the ready.

Suddenly, he halted. There was a rustling sound from somewhere in the bushes. He heard the sound of whistling ...

The Sontaran fired and the blaster bolt seared through the bushes. After a moment, the whistling started up again, from a slightly different direction. The Sontaran forced his way into the bushes determined to catch sight of his quarry. A dense clump of vines barred his way, and he thrust his way through them. Or rather, he tried to ...

Suddenly the vines came to furious life, winding hundreds of tentacles around him in a crushing grip. Arms pinioned, unable to reach his blaster, the Sontaran struggled desperately creating a tremendous racket as his heavy limbs flailed at the greenery.

The Doctor popped out from behind a nearby bush and observed the struggle with benign interest. 'I can see you two are getting on very well,' he said, and hurried on his way.


The Sontaran was still struggling, though more feebly, when Stor and Kelner came into the conservatory. Stor raised his communicator, made an adjustment, and switched it on. There was a high-pitched electronic hum. Paralysed by the high-frequency sound wave, the vine-plant's tentacles went limp. The Sontaran trooper staggered out.

Stor looked at the trooper dispassionately. 'You will follow this Time Lord and destroy the power unit he will show you. Report to me in the Panopticon when you have succeeded.' Stor produced a grenade from his belt, and checked its timer.

The trooper saluted, and followed Kelner from the conservatory. Stor stood motionless for a moment. He took off his helmet, and stood breathing hard, as if the strain of the long chase was beginning to tell even on him.

So many delays, so many frustrations, victory always so close, yet always snatched away at the last moment. His ship, and the whole Sontaran battle fleet trapped outside the barrier. He had conquered a planet, and now he had to hold it with only a handful of men.

Stor's lipless mouth tightened, and his little red eyes blazed with anger. Dok-tor! Always Dok-tor! He would kill the Dok-tor and then all would be well. If necessary, he would destroy all Gallifrey to ensure the Doctor's death. Stor hurried away.

Kelner led the Sontaran trooper into a small but elegant gallery. Masterpieces from many planets lined the walls, statues and busts were scattered here and there about the room.

Kelner looked around admiringly. 'Beautiful, isn't it?'

The Sontaran said nothing. Beauty is of no interest to Sontarans, since it has no function in war. Indeed, to a Sontaran war *is* beauty. 'What is this place?'

'An ancilliary power station. How like the Doctor to conceal its function with beauty!'

Kelner went over to the largest statue, a robed female figure in the style of ancient Greece. He opened a small hatch in the side of the statue's plinth, and pressed an off-switch. 'Now, try your tracer.'

The trooper took the device from his belt, switched on and studied the readings. 'The humanoids are

135

three levels below!' he announced triumphantly. 'We shall go and destroy them!'


In the workshop, the Doctor, Borusa and Andred stood watching Rodan as she put the final touches to a complex, rifle-like weapon. K9 stood smugly by, like an instructor watching a prize pupil at work.

'Finished?' said the Doctor.

'Yes. It is finished.'

The Doctor snapped his fingers. 'Wake up, Rodan. Give me the Great Key.'

Rodan blinked, produced the Key from her belt-pouch and handed it to the Doctor.

The Doctor picked up the gun and stood for a moment, Great Key in one hand, gun in the other.

Suddenly Borusa understood what was happening and an expression of horror came over his face. 'No!' he whispered. 'No!'

The Doctor's face was stern. 'You know how helpless we are against the Sontarans, Chancellor.'

'I forbid you to use that weapon, Doctor. It should never have been created.'

'What is it?' asked Leela, curiously.

'The ultimate weapon,' said the Doctor simply. 'The De-mat gun.'

Rodan was as horrified as Borusa. 'But that's impossible. All knowledge of that weapon is forbidden, by Rassilon's decree.'

'But the information was still there, stored in the Matrix. K9 passed it on to you, and you built the gun under hypnosis.'

The Doctor looked down at the weapon. 'Now I have only to arm it. This is why the Great Key remained hidden for so long.'

The Doctor slipped the key into a slot in the butt

of the weapon and snapped it home. The gun seemed to throb with energy in his hands. For a moment he felt the exhilaration of total power—and realised why Rassilon had ordered that the weapon should be forbidden. 'With this weapon, I could rule the Universe, eh, Chancellor?'

'Is that what you want? Destroy it, Doctor! Destroy all knowledge of it, or it will throw us back to the darkest age!'

'No!' whispered a harsh voice from the doorway. 'It will take us forward, to a new age of Sontaran conquest.'

The Doctor turned. A Sontaran trooper was in the doorway, Kelner close behind him.

As the Sontaran raised his blaster the Doctor fired the De-mat gun. The Sontaran vanished, abolished from existence.

The Doctor swung the weapon to cover Kelner. 'Where is Commander Stor.'

Kelner didn't reply.

'Kill him, Leela,' said the Doctor casually. Leela drew her knife and moved forward.

'The Panopticon,' screamed Kelner. 'He's in the Panopticon. I think he's got some kind of bomb.'

Horrified, the Doctor dashed for the door.


Stor had almost finished his task. The fusion grenade was primed and ready, placed squarely in the centre of the dais. He straightened up to see the Doctor standing over him, a strange weapon in his hand.

'Wait, Stor.'

'This final action will provide me with great pleasure, Dok-tor.'

'You'll destroy yourself and your men, as well as us ...'

137

'It is an honour to die for the glorious Sontaran Empire.'

'The power of a block hole is trapped beneath us. Explode that grenade and you'll destroy the entire planet.'

'And all the Time Lords on it!'

'You'll set off a chain reaction that will blow up your own battle fleet.'

'We have many battle fleets. If we cannot conquer you, Time Lord, we shall destroy you! Goodbye— Dok-tor!'

Stor triggered the grenade.

## 15

## The Wisdom of Rassilon

In the same moment, the Doctor raised the De-mat gun and fired.

Stor vanished and the exploding grenade vanished, too. Somehow the energies released by atomic grenade and De-mat gun blended, merged, and cancelled each other out.

The force of the energy-collision flung the Doctor back across the dais and dropped him unconscious on the ground.

In the vast, shadowy Panopticon, everything was quiet. Stor was gone. The fusion-grenade was gone. Even the De-mat gun had disappeared.

All that remained of it was the triggering device, the Great Key of Rassilon. It lay on the floor, close to the outstretched hand of the Doctor, who lay still as death.

The shock of the explosion was felt even in the TARDIS workshop. For a time, Borusa, Andred, Rodan, Leela and K9 waited, wondering what had happened, and what they should do. They heard slow, heavy footsteps, coming towards the workshop door.

Borusa lifted the staser, Leela drew her knife.

The door opened and the Doctor stood swaying in the doorway, exhausted, yet somehow relieved, as if some great weight had been lifted from his shoulders.

Leela ran to help him. 'Doctor, are you all right?'

The Doctor beamed at her. 'Hello, Leela.' He looked at Borusa. 'What on Earth are you doing here, Borusa?'

'Your Excellency?'

'My Excellency? Is this some kind of a joke, Borusa? You never used to make jokes! And why am I wearing this thing?' He unfastened the Sash of Rassilion, and stared at it in amazement.

'But Your Excellency,' said Borusa, 'don't you remember your induction as President?'

'My induction? *Me*, President?' Clearly, the Doctor remembered no such thing.

'And the Vardans?'

'What Vardans?'

'The Sontarans?'

'What Sontarans?'

Borusa put his hands on the Doctor's shoulders. 'Doctor, you have just saved Gallifrey.'

'Have I really?' said the Doctor delightedly.

'What do you say to that Leela?'

Leela looked at Borusa. 'His mind has gone,' she whispered.

Borusa smiled. 'No,' he said gently, 'only his memory. It is better so. It is the wisdom of Rassilon.'


Some time later a small group of Time Lords and Outsiders led by Nesbin and Borusa assembled around the TARDIS. As usual the Doctor had firmly rejected any thought of official thanks or a farewell reception, and had insisted on a quiet departure.

He paused embarrassed in the TARDIS doorway. The Doctor had always hated farewells. 'Well, goodbye everybody. Come on, Leela.'

Leela didn't move. 'I am staying Doctor.'

'Staying here? Why?'

Andred was standing beside Leela, and she reached

140

out and took his hand. In Leela's tribe, females as well as males could choose their mates, and Leela had chosen. Andred looked pleased, but a little startled.

'Oh I see,' said the Doctor thoughtfully.

'Doctor, I hope——' began Andred.

'I'm sure you hope,' said the Doctor solemnly. 'Don't worry, she'll look after you. She's very good with a knife. Come on K9.'

'Negative, Master.'

'You're staying too?'

'Affirmative.'

'Why?'

'To look after the Mistress—Master.'

The Doctor nodded. Clearly an automaton could have feelings after all.

A little sadly the Doctor opened the TARDIS door.

Leela called. 'Doctor!'

'Yes, Leela?'

'I'll miss you, Doctor.'

'I'll miss you too—savage!'

Raising his hand in a farewell salute to Borusa, the Doctor went inside the TARDIS and closed the door.

A minute or two later there was a wheezing, groaning sound and the blue police box dematerialised.

Leela turned to K9. 'Will he be lonely?'

'Insufficient data, Mistress.' But K9's tail antenna dropped sadly.

Andred took Leela's hand, and they walked away.

K9 glided after them.


In the TARDIS control room, the Doctor wandered around the console, adjusting the controls here and there, and telling himself he quite liked it on his own.

He didn't believe himself. Suddenly, a thought

141

struck him. He opened a storage locker and pulled out an enormous cardboard box. On it was stencilled 'K9, Mark II'. The Doctor smiled.

Anything any other scientist could do, he could do better. He'd designed and assembled the parts for a new improved K9 some time ago, though he'd kept the box hidden for fear of hurting the feelings of the original.

Happily, the Doctor opened the box and set to work.

## 'Doctor Who'

| | | | |
|---|---|---|---|
| Δ | 0426114558 | Terrance Dicks<br>**DOCTOR WHO AND THE ABOMINABLE**<br>**SNOWMEN** | **70p** |
| Δ | 0426200373 | Terrance Dicks<br>**DOCTOR WHO AND THE**<br>**ANDROID INVASION** | **60p** |
| Δ | 0426116313 | Ian Marter<br>**DOCTOR WHO AND THE**<br>**ARK IN SPACE** | **70p** |
| Δ | 0426116747 | Terrance Dicks<br>**DOCTOR WHO AND THE**<br>**BRAIN OF MORBIUS** | **60p** |
| Δ | 0426110250 | Terrance Dicks<br>**DOCTOR WHO AND THE**<br>**CARNIVAL OF MONSTERS** | **70p** |
| Δ | 042611471X | Malcolm Hulke<br>**DOCTOR WHO AND THE**<br>**CAVE-MONSTERS** | **70p** |
| Δ | 0426117034 | Terrance Dicks<br>**DOCTOR WHO AND THE**<br>**CLAWS OF AXOS** | **70p** |
| Δ | 0426113160 | David Whitaker<br>**DOCTOR WHO AND THE**<br>**CRUSADERS** | **70p** |
| Δ | 0426114981 | Brian Hayles<br>**DOCTOR WHO AND THE**<br>**CURSE OF PELADON** | **70p** |
| Δ | 042611244X | Terrance Dicks<br>**DOCTOR WHO AND THE**<br>**DALEK INVASION OF EARTH** | **70p** |
| Δ | 0426103807 | Terrance Dicks<br>**DOCTOR WHO AND THE**<br>**DAY OF THE DALEKS** | **70p** |
| Δ | 0426101103 | David Whitaker<br>**DOCTOR WHO AND THE**<br>**DALEKS** | **70p** |
| Δ | 0426119657 | Terrance Dicks<br>**DOCTOR WHO AND THE**<br>**DEADLY ASSASSIN** | **60p** |
| Δ | 0426200063 | Terrance Dicks<br>**DOCTOR WHO AND THE**<br>**FACE OF EVIL** | **70p** |
| Δ | 0426112601 | Terrance Dicks<br>**DOCTOR WHO AND THE**<br>**GENESIS OF THE DALEKS** | **60p** |

† For sale in Britain and Ireland only.
\* Not for sale in Canada.
♦ Film & T.V. tie-ins.

If you enjoyed this book and would like to have information sent to you about other TARGET titles, write to the address below.

*You will also receive:*
A FREE TARGET BADGE!
Based on the TARGET BOOKS symbol — see front cover of this book — this attractive three-colour badge, pinned to your blazer-lapel or jumper, will excite the interest and comment of all your friends!

*and you will be further entitled to:*
FREE ENTRY INTO THE TARGET DRAW!
All you have to do is cut off the coupon below, write on it your name and address in *block capitals,* and pin it to your letter. Twice a year, in June, and December, coupons will be drawn 'from the hat' and the winner will receive a complete year's set of TARGET books.

Write to:

# TARGET BOOKS
## 44 Hill Street
## London W1X 8LB

cut here

Full name .................................................

Address.................................................

.................................................

.................................................

Age......................

PLEASE ENCLOSE A SELF-ADDRESSED STAMPED ENVELOPE WITH YOUR COUPON!